I0761846

UNDERWORLD

Underworld is a work of fiction. References to real people, events, establishments, organizations, or locales are intended only to provide the sense of authenticity and are use fictitiously. All other characters, all incidents, dialogue are drawn from the author's imagination and are not to be seen as real.

Published by Dark Titan Publishing. A division of Dark Titan Entertainment.

Also available in eBook.

Dark Titan Universe is a branch of Dark Titan Entertainment.

Hardcover ISBN: 978-1-7376143-3-3
eBook ISBN: 978-1-7376143-4-0

darktitanentertainment.com

WORKS BY TY'RON W. C. ROBINSON II

BOOKS/SHORT STORIES

DARK TITAN UNIVERSE SAGA

MAIN SERIES

Dark Titan Knights
The Resistance Protocol
Tales of the Scattered
Tales of the Numinous
Day of Octagon
Crossbreed
Heaven's Called
The Oranos Imperative
Underworld

Forthcoming

Magicks and Mysticism
The Resistance vs. The Enforcement Order

COLLECTIONS

Dark Titan Omnibus: Volume 1
Dark Titan Omnibus: Volume 2
Dark Titan One-Shot Collection

SPIN-OFFS

In A Glass of Dawn: The Casebook of Travis Vail
Maveth: Bloodsport
The Curse of The Mutant-Thing

Forthcoming

Trail of Vengeance
War of The Thunder Gods
Maveth vs. The Swordman

ONE-SHOTS

Maveth, The Death-Bringer
Mystery of The Mutant-Thing
Shade & Switchblade
Retribution of Cain
The Mythologists
Ambush Bot
Kang-Zhu
Cheeseburger Man
Tessa Balthazar

THE HAUNTED CITY SAGA

The Legendary Warslinger: The Haunted City I
Battle of Astolat: A Haunted City Prequel (KOBO Exclusive)
Redemption of the Lost: The Haunted City II
Consequences of the Suffering: The Haunted City III (Forthcoming)

SYMBOLUM VENATORES

Symbolum Venatores: The Gabriel Kane Collection
Hod: A Symbolum Venatores Book
Symbolum Venatores: War of The Two Kingdoms
Symbolum Venatores: Elrad's Chronicles
Symbolum Venatores: Mystery of the Magician (Forthcoming)
Symbolum Venatores: Twilight of the Gods (Forthcoming)

EVERWAR UNIVERSE

EverWar Universe: Knights & Lords

EverWar Universe: The Damned Ones (Forthcoming)

PRODIGIOUS WORLDS

Mark Porter of Argoron

Raiders of Vanok

Praxus of Lithonia (Forthcoming)

FRIGHTENED! SERIES

Frightened!: The Beginning

Frightened!: The Light Sky (Forthcoming)

INSTINCTS SERIES

Lost in Shadows: Remastered

Instincts: Point Hope (Forthcoming)

Shadow in the Mirror: Instincts II (Forthcoming)

DARK TITAN'S THE DEAD DAYS

Accounts of The Dead Days

Brand New Day: The Dead Days I (Forthcoming)

OTHER BOOKS

The Book of The Elect

The Extended Age Omnibus

The Horde

The Eleventh Hour: A Chevah Mythos Story

The Supreme Pursuer: Darkness of the Hunt

Massacre in the Dusk

THE DARK TITAN AUDIO EXPERIENCE PODCAST

Season 1: Introductions

Season 2: In a Glass of Dawn

Season 2.5: Accounts of The Dead Days

Season 3: Battle For Astolat

Season 4: Hallow Sword: Cursed

TY'RON W. C. ROBINSON II

CONTENTS

DARK TITAN UNIVERSE ONE SHOT: KANG-ZHU

Moving through the small area of Mass City, Kang-Zhu traveled outward pass the city and deeper into the Fable Mountains. Upon his arrival at the mountains, he found the ruins of an ancient temple. Not surprised by its appearance, Kang-Zhu entered the area, finding more than one temple. Three were decimated into the ground while two remained standing. However, one was weathered down throughout history, as its beams wound crack in the silent night. The secondary temple was not weakened, yet stood strong. Intriguing to Kang-Zhu and his mission. Walking toward the temple, fire lit up across the temple entrance across its walls. Kang-Zhu paused.

"This is the place."

Kang-Zhu approached the temple doors. Their height stood over ten feet and Kang-Zhu pushed them open, unveiling a much larger room and standing inside were a dozen men, cloaked in black robes. Their faces hidden by shrouded masks. Kang-Zhu stood before them as the temple doors shut.

"Where is your master?" Kang-Zhu asked. "Speak up."

The robed men said nothing. Kang-Zhu stretched out his arms and from his hands emitted embers, glowing with a green hue. Kang-Zhu clapped his hands together, causing a shockwave through the air, stumbling the robed men from their frozen state.

"I will not ask again." Kang-Zhu said.

Two of the robed men stepped from their position, rushing toward Kang-Zhu with their fists. Kang blocked the incoming blows and retuned them with his palm. The men stood back as the others entered into the fight. Now Kang was against six men on his own, blocking each of their attacks. From punches, kicks, jabs, and palms. Kang smirked and blew the men back with a gust of energy. The men paused, seeing the hue once again. They knew it was Kang's chi.

"I'm not finished yet." Kang-Zhu grinned.

Kang removed his leather trench coat, unveiling his battle attire. A vest mixed with the colors of emerald and ruby. Forearm gauntlets which glistened like gold. Kevlar-linen pants with leather-padded boots. Kang-Zhu stood in his stance, welcoming all the robed men into the fight. The men all attacked Kang-Zhu. Within the battle, Kang-Zhu charged up his energy and attacked each of the robed men with kicks in precision. He moved with such speed, the men weren't able to catch up to his attacks. Once they caught up, each of them were tossed back and collapsed onto the temple grounds. Kang sighed as he saw three of the men rise up, ready to fight once again.

"Are you sure?" Kang-Zhu asked.

Once Kang made his move to finish them ff, a cloaked figure emerged from above, taking out the three robed men with a staff. Kang paused himself, seeing the figure holding the staff. Kang gazed closer, seeing the staff was in fact a naginata. The figure revealed their face by removing the hood.

"Who are you?" Kang asked.

"My name is Kimmiko Vantez. Others call me Gozen."

"I see. And why have you come here? To finish off my adversaries?"

"They are not only your enemies. They are also mine."

"Do tell."

"I've been tracking these Warriors of the Claw for some time. Ever since I came across a few of their agents in Retropolis. I often wondered why they were here. My question now is who are they working for."

"I might have an answer to that."

Gozen turned back toward Kang-Zhu, removing the blood from her blade.

"Give me a name."

"I don't have a name." Kang-Zhu said. "But, I have a location."

"Which is?"

"Chicago."

"And what is your source?"

"My travels haven taken me across many places in search of my own abilities. I have yet to master them and this cult of warriors is the key to finding my answers. Last I learned, they operate by an unseen force which moves throughout Chicago. Not sure of its one individual or an entire clan."

"Then, it settles it, I'll contact my associates and inform them of my travels to Chicago."

"Sure. But, I will be going as well."

Gozen looked back at Kang-Zhu with curiosity moving through her eyes..

"What is your name?"

"Kang-Zhu."

Gozen nodded. Placing he sheath over her blade.

"*Upright King.*"

"How did you know?"

"I've been around this line of work since childhood."

Gozen whistles, revealing a horse coming through the mist. He jumped on, nodding toward Kang-Zhu.

"I'm sure you are aware of the others in Chicago."

"I am not."

"Very well. Once you arrive there, you will be met by them. Take it as a test and not a threat."

"I will."

Gozen rode off through the moonlight as Kang clenched his hands with the hue emitted once again. Kang smashed his hands into the ground, creating a wave of energy over him. He picked up his hands from the ground and was gone as the energy evaporated.

THE ASTONISHING VOLTAGE: FROZEN FRONTS

I

A COLD FRONT

Steve Walker sat inside his room, thinking on the past events which have transpired since the rise of the heroes. From making himself known to the world as The Astonishing Voltage to saving Los Angeles from King Marc, aligning with Doctor Fortune, Kular the Aqua-Barbarian, and The Unstoppable Beast against Sinister Judge to form the Protectors, even his rough encounter with Sonicwave, all up to the point of clashing with The Resistance and facing the might of Oranos and his army from Blachole. Steve took some time to collect himself after the battle in Blachole against Oranos, Thrudhawk, Dominix, and Dagard.

From there, Steve geared up and headed out into the city as The Voltage. Moving through the city like a running bolt of lightning in the air with flashes of his full being showing within every microsecond. Moving at such speed, Voltage caught several robberies and took the criminals to prison in a short time, startling the officers as the robbers were brought in. The Voltage took the moments during his run and while flowing through the air in his electric form, he felt a strange and peculiar chill. Reverting to his human form, he landed atop a roof and rubbed his arms.

"Cold. Wait? How is it cold? It's L.A. in the summer."

Voltage looked around the air, not seeing anything which could connect to the sudden chill. He even gazed up to the sky, only seeing the clear blue sky. He shook his head and brushed the chilling sense from his body and went back into the city, forming back into the moving in lighting. However, lurking within the city was a figure. Which moved with the cold as it lumbered into the darkness of the city.

II

RESPONSIBILITIES

Later throughout the day, Steve went and spent time with his friends out in the city. While they sat down for lunch, Steve began to hear them talk of the heroes roaming throughout the world. Gregg continued to speak about The Resistance while Ava went on about the Voltage. Steve remained silent. Shaking his head slightly to avoid the conversation. Emily had paused and asked Steve what he thought of the heroes. He caught himself, staring at his friends.

"They're alright."

Ava gave him the side-eye while Gregg shook his head, smacking on his sandwich. Emily only smiled. Steve continued to tell them the heroes were around for a much greater cause and purpose. To which Ava replied with a gesture of the Voltage's accomplishments. Gregg paused himself, listening to Ava's praise.

"There's no way the Voltage can match up to Taltus."

"That's not a fair comparison." Ava replied. "We know Taltus isn't human."

"But, he's a hero. Can you imagine standing next to someone like him. A being from another dimension. From a place where gods dwell."

"What kind of gods?" Emily wondered. "I'm not familiar on the Taltus figure."

"He's from Mount Olympus." Gregg said. "Or a place on the mountain. Something like that."

"Doesn't exactly make him fit in with the gods." Ava added.

"Then, that means the Greek gods exist?" Emily asked.

"Of course!" Gregg yelled. "How else could Taltus be here if not for them."

The air had quickly changed from the summer air to the chilling cold. Steve stood up, looking around. His friends began to notice the cold as they shivered. Gregg began asking what was happening while Steve was calm. Neither was he taken aback by the cold or was he shaking.

"I need to go." Steve told his friends.

"Go?" Ava said. "Go where?"

"I have some other matters to attend to. Just came up is all."

Ava nodded slightly as the look in her eyes told Steve everything. He went and left the area just as his friends were preparing themselves to do the same. The civilians around them began to flee inside the neighboring stores. Around the corner, Steve went into an alley and began changing his apparel from his civilian gear to his Voltage suit. Sliding the mask on last, the electrical flowed over his body like a charge. He leaped into the air and streaked like lightning. Bolting through the air, his static electricity began to tick from the cold. Tracing it in the area, Voltage came to a stop on the rooftop of a building, looking over he saw a tall figure, layered in glacier ice from head to toe. Yet, the figure wore a black suit which appeared to gleam like Kevlar. Voltage watched as the icy figure was manipulating the cold air into solid beams of ice and setting them aside.

"What's this guy's deal?" Voltage asked.

He leaped to the concrete as the figure turned to see him.

"You must be new around here." Voltage said. "L.A. doesn't get this much cold. Especially during the summer days."

"Keep walking, hero."

"I can't. Because you see you're causing a disturbance. So, I'm gonna have to get you out of here."

The figure's hands sparked with ice as the chilling cold surrounded them both. The Voltage held his stance, yet he began to feel the air piercing through his suit. Shaking himself, electricity covered his body. The icy figure nodded.

"You seem to have a defense mechanism built into you."

"It's kind of a gift."

"A gift that will be ruined."

The icy figure blasted a beam of ice toward Voltage. The hero twirled in the air while sparking with lightning.

"Nice move, Frostface!"

Landing back onto his feet, Voltage fired back two bolts of lightning, shaking the figure. Bolting with speed, Voltage air-kicked the figure to the ground, crashing him into several of his own ice-columns. The figure laughed, confusing the young hero.

"They were right about your prowess. Your skill. Yet, you've never faced one such as I."

The figure shocked Voltage with a blast that triggered an almost seizure-like effect. The Voltage collapsed onto the ground, shaking as the figure left the scene by forming his body into nothing but small fragments of ice. Once the entity had vanished from the scene, the cold fizzled out and Voltage regained himself. Picking himself up from the ground and taking deep breathes. He looked at his arms, seeing the suit torn from frostbite.

"No."

Looking at his shut in its entirely, it was damaged. Covered in tiny layers of ice, he removed his suit and streaked into the sky, returning to his apartment.

III

AN UPGRADE

Steve drove out to the outskirts of Los Angeles, pulling up on a small cabin which was rough to see from several drives afar. He knocked on the door and waited. Once it opened, Steve saw his friend. Smiles on both their faces as they shook hands and hugged.

"Still in one piece."

"As I'll ever be, Rax."

"Come on inside and tell me why you've come to visit me."

Inside the cabin, Steve saw over a dozen computers. Desktops and laptops. On the tables nearing the kitchen were three tablets plugged in, some pizza boxes scattered across the couch. Steve scoffed.

"You don't do much cleaning, huh?"

"It's just me here. Besides, there's so much work to be done."

Steve sat at the coffee table, which was standing next to the couch. Rax sat down in front of him and extended his hands. Steve was unsure. Rax shrugged his shoulders while fixing his glasses.

"What?" Steve asked.

"Why have you come here?"

"Oh. I need a favor. A quick one."

"A quick favor? Must be something that can be done in less than an hour."

"That would be good. I know your skills are useful. Especially the way you do things. You have pulp speed."

"That's good to know. So, what do you need my help with?"

"I need a new suit."

"New suit? Why? The old yellow and blue isn't working in style anymore?"

"No. there's a new threat to the city. Some frost face looking guy. My suit isn't capable of standing up to him in combat. His freezing ability go right through the fabric. I never prepared to fight against a walking iceman."

"Well, a hero always prepares."

"This is California." Steve noted. "You tell me the last time there was a deep freeze in the state. Let alone a blizzard."

"Fair point." Rax replied, wiping the pizza crumbs off his chin. "Well here, I'll get something done for you in no time."

"I would appreciate it, Rax. Honestly."

"I know you would. Also, I have a question for you."

"What kind of question?"

"Are the others as stubborn as the people say they are?"

"The others?"

"The other heroes? The one's you met."

"Not all of them. The Swordman keeps to himself. Taltus is a born leader, whether he knows it or not. Nano Man is as arrogant as they come. Theus is a living god, not sure where he is now."

"I heard about your groupings with that doctor guy in D.C. as well. Including your little spout with that walking robot."

"You're talking about Doctor Fortune and Octagon. In that order."

"I would love to meet them someday. Perhaps, I can give them a helping hand."

"The way you do things, Rax, I'm sure you'll meet them eventually. Hopefully, it's on a good call and not some kind of takeover one."

"Yeah. Won't we all." Rax smiled.

"You need me to do anything for you regarding the suit? Diagrams and whatnot?"

"No need. I saved the diagrams from the first suit. The one I will construct for you will not take as long as you think. Just needs a thicker hide is all."

"So, I'll just wait here until you're finished."

"Of course." Rax responded. "What else were you going to do."

Steve laughed as Rax took the diagrams from the scanner on the nearby table and walked into the back of the cabin where he had an arsenal of uniforms and equipment on standby. Steve looked and saw it and before he could walk closer, the TV flashed with the news loudly echoing. He turned to the TV and what he saw was chaos taking place on Hollywood Boulevard. The news began broadcasting the iceman's sudden arrival as he was blasting the entire area with ice, freezing the civilians caught in the sights.

"Whenever you get finished with that suit will be great." Steve said.

"Don't rush me, bro." Rax yelled. "This takes great skill."

IV

A BATTLE FOR THE CAMERAS

Continuing in Hollywood Blvd, the ice entity continued his ravage against the people. Freezing those who come across his gaze. The news continued their broadcast as the entity saw them. Moving with a slow walk, his eyes were on them. Piercing a glint of red mixed with the icy blue. From his hands formed whirlwinds of ice. The ice twirling in his hands began to take form. Their shape was undetermined by only a moment's look. Standing still, he raised his right hand in the air as the whirlwind intensified. The news reporters all ran for cover as the sky rained down hail in the form of sharp daggers.

"Get into the buildings now!" One reporter yelled toward the people.

"Isn't this what you crave?!" The entity spoke. "You sought some saving time from your summer season. I give you a small taste of the winter. Of what's to come in only a moment's notice!"

The ice daggers shattered against the windows of the buildings. Most of the people crowded themselves into the theaters, taking a look out through the windows. The entity walked through the open road with his hand still raised above. The storm continued for nearly five minutes before he called it to cease. The entity laughed at the destruction around him. Cars destroyed and dented from the ice. Windows shattered and cracked. The small sounds of people's fear echoing through the silent street.

"Where is your hero now?"

"The people began to look around for the Voltage, yet he was not around. Some had hope and others began to accept the possibility of the Voltage not coming to their safety. The people in-between those beliefs began to stand up. Coming out from the buildings where they hid and walked into the street toward the entity. Hearing the cracking of ice behind him, he turned to see the civilians standing and staring. In their hands, some held baseball bats. Others carried hammers. The entity scoffed at their determined will.

"You seek to attack me?!"

"You've caused enough trouble here." One civilian said, holding the bat. "Best you go ahead and take your leave."

"Or what? You and your little clan will eliminate me yourselves? You believe you have what it takes to defeat me? Someone as powerful as I?"

"If not all of us, one of us will."

"Very well." The entity spoke as the storm began to reform in the sky. "Take your best shot!"

The first civilian lunged toward the entity with the baseball bat. With a swing, the bat froze in the air from the entity's own temperature. Seeing the bat's remains shattering onto the ground, the entity grabbed the civilian by his neck and began to slowly freeze him. The other civilians charged toward the entity with whatever they carried. Stepping at almost two feet toward him, they froze in an instant. Solid ice covered their bodies.

"No match for someone as me."

"What about me?" A voice echoed through the air.

The entity turned around and looked up atop one of the buildings and saw the Voltage standing. The Voltage fired two lightning bolts toward the entity, stumbling him in his steps as he dropped the civilian. The civilians thanked Voltage before making an escape. The Voltage fired more lightning bolts, shattering the ice from suffocating the others. Telling them to evacuate the area, they did not hesitate. The entity looked up and blasted an ice bean against Voltage, crashing into his chest, causing him to fall to the ground. Only for him to catch his balance and land on his feet. When Voltage had stood up, the entity noticed some different.

"Your wear. It's changed."

Voltage looked at his suit and to the entity's surprise, it absorbed the ice blast. The suit was detailed in the same fashion as his original suit, but this one was coated in armor. An armor which was capable of absorbing the entity's ice blasts. Yet, this suit was not in the same color scheme as his original, but in a light blue and yellow. His eyes were a bright yellow and sparks began to flow across his limbs.

"So, you've gained an advantage. Tell me how you've achieved such a feat?"

"Best I don't share my tactics. That's kind of a non-disclosure thing."

"And you think I cannot pierce through your new armor? You haven't even felt the fill force of my power."

"Then, what are you waiting for?' Voltage asked with cockiness. "Get to it."

The entity screamed with rage, firing ice blasts from both his hands toward the Voltage. Moving with swiftness of speed and lightning, Voltage dodged the blasts and retaliated with several lightning blasts of his own. Striking the entity in his chest and tapping into his own power. The entity paused himself, touching the wound on his chest as the Voltage stopped like a lightning strike.

"Something wrong?" Voltage asked. "Did I do something I shouldn't have?"

"You will not win this battle!"

"I think I will."

Voltage charged himself up as he moved toward the entity. The two charged up with their own attacks and within that mere second, they clashed. Electricity against ice. The clash created a shockwave, which moved through Hollywood Boulevard. Blasting them both back from one another. Silence had surrounded the area as Voltage rose up from the debris around him, shaking the ice from his body as electricity moved across him with flashes of lightning. Looking ahead, he saw the entity laid out on the ground. Voltage walked over to him and checked his pulse as best he could. For he had a large glacier of ice surrounding his head and neck.

"He doesn't appear to be dead." Voltage said. "So, that's good."

From there, the police had arrived and apprehended the entity. Taking him to the same facility as King Marc. Being sent in, the city proclaimed the entity to be known as Frostface. A name which was chosen by Voltage himself. Once the city had regained its normal summer temperature and the streets were cleared of ice, Voltage reverted back to his original suit. Keeping the self-proclaimed 'Voltage-Armor' in a case inside Rax's cabin.

While on a patrol through the city, a continuing commotion of screams called to Voltage in an alleyway. Making his way toward the sound, he landed on the ground. Finding no one. The alley was clear. Leaving him confused as he scratched his head.

"I know I heard screaming. I know I did."

Hearing the screams again, Voltage looked forward, seeing a woman tussling with a mugger who sought to take her purse. Moving with lighting speed, Voltage snatched the purse and super-kicked the mugger, knocking him out in a second. The woman was stunned as Voltage returned her purse.

"Thank you for saving me."

"It's my job." Voltage replied. "Just do me a favor and avoid alleys. Ones like this. They're always bound for trouble."

"I will. Thank you again."

The woman fled the alley as Voltage waved her off. Seeking to leave the alley, Voltage was confronted by three men. Ninjas who were cloaked in their uniforms.

"Uh. What's going on here?" Voltage asked. "Are you guys from some kind of karate school or something? You seeking new recruits, because I might be interested."

The three ninjas attacked Voltage from all sides. Eventually getting him to the ground where they stomped him. Sighing from annoyance, Voltage jolted himself up to his feet and kicked one to the ground. The remaining two retrieved their comrade and tossed a flash grenade to the ground. Once the blindness was removed, Voltage looked around the alley to see the ninjas had vanished. The one thing Voltage managed to capture was their insignia. The letter W with a large scratch across.

"Who were they?" Voltage asked, taking his leave from the alley and back into the city.

BIONIC RAGE: COURSED AGENDA

I

BECOMING A HERO

The warehouse echoed with gunfire and shouting voices. The men clad in armor ran down the corridors shooting back into the shadows. Two of the men rushed into the darkness with their guns and within seconds, they were flung through the air, crashing into the walls. From the shadows emerged Dameon Mason, now know to the public as the Bionic Rage. The men retaliated with more gunfire and Dameon grinned. He raised his arms, clicking and loading before they fired back rounds. His arms blasted like a tommy gun, killing the men in seconds. Dameon continued his attack on the others within the warehouse. Eventually eliminating all the armed men inside. Afterwards, he searched the place and discovered crates of weapons. Stamped on the crates was the name 'Vargas'. Dameon sighed.

"He's still continuing his operations. Even while behind bars."

Dameon went ahead and destroyed the weapons and the crates. Causing an explosion to echo around the surrounding areas where the warehouse stood. Dameon walked out of the warehouse as the entire building collapsed. With the debris flying across the sky and crashing around him, Dameon took one look back at the decimation warehouse. His work was done. His feet pressured against the ground and Dameon took off into the morning sky.

II

WELCOME YOUR FEARS

Once the city felt itself protected and secure with Bionic Rage's aid, crime began to have a tumble. Less criminals attempted to make themselves known in fear of being confronted by Dameon. His reputation spread throughout the city. The criminals and mob bosses knew Bionic Rage would kill them if they ever made contact. Fear consumes them to the point where they chose to keep their operations in the shadows rather than out in the day. Meanwhile, Dameon remained at his home uninterrupted by those who caught a glimpse of him out in the city. Brad and Claire would continually visit him and inform him of circumstances across the city. Elsewhere, Nathan Armstrong began to build an act that would protect Dameon against any federal laws, as some officials sought to bring Dameon in for vigilantism. Nathan told them such actions against Dameon would ensure conflict and Bionic Rage isn't afraid to fight those in authority to secure his freedom.

Yet, during one cloudy day, the skies over Detroit transformed from the thin grey to a dark orange. The civilians all gathered outside to see the sudden change. Others went ahead and prepared to evacuate as orange clouds are necessarily natural. From the clouds bolted orange and red lightning strikes. The people fled as quickly as possible. Leading to the news to broadcast the strange occurrence. Sitting at his home, working on his limbs by loading them up with shotgun rounds, Dameon saw the tint of the orange glistened across a window. Hearing his phone ringing, he answered it.

"What's happening?"

"Dameon, something's wrong." Brad said on the other side. "The skies are orange and there's lightning. This is strange. I've never seen these kinds of clouds before."

"I'm not certain as to how I can help." Dameon responded. "Has anyone checked the weather?"

"Today was supposed to be a stormy day. But, not like this."

"Well, it appears the forecast was not as they said, is it?"

His arms locked. The gears turning as the rounds within his forearms began to move in place. He stood up and exited the home, gazing out toward the city from the distance. His bionic legs began to brighten as he lifted himself into the air, flying toward the city and the orange cloud. Reaching the city, one of the lightning bolts struck Dameon, causing him to lose his balance in the air. His bionic limbs going in and out of power as was his reactor. His eyes began to fade as he took a deep breath and before hitting the pavement, his limbs regained strength and held him up. Although, whole falling, Dameon had breathed in some of the cloud and from there, all he could see around him was death. Dead civilians, dead soldiers, and in the sky, crashing planes and hovering missiles. the cloud had caused a trigger effect into Dameon's psyche. He knew what the images were and collapsed to the ground, holding himself. Dameon knew he was witnessing past memories of his life before he became Bionic Rage.

While Dameon was crouched in a corner near an alleyway in the city, civilians saw him, but were very hesitant to approach as they feared he would harm them if they touched him. While they watched, a vehicle drove up and out of it exited Claire as she saw Dameon on the ground, hearing his faint yelps. Sitting in the car in the driver's seat was Brad.

"What's wrong with him?!" Brad asked.

"I don't know. He's not physically harmed. It's something else."

"They're... they're all dead." Dameon mumbled.

"What?" Claire asked. "Who's dead?"

"All of them... all of them."

"Look, Dameon, we're here to take you home." Claire said, looking back at Brad. "Come on. Steady."

Claire yelled at the civilians who were standing in her way as she walked Dameon to the car. He entered as they drove out of the city.

III

SCARED?

Making their return to Dameon's home, they sat him on the couch and once they did, Claire noticed an orange hue in his eyes.

"What is that?"

"What's what?" Brad questioned.

"They're a orange cloud in his eyes. Looks just like the ones above the city."

"He was flying in the air. Might've came into contact with it."

"But, that doesn't explain why he's so fearful. They're something else at work here."

Dameon was shaking. His forearm covered in sweat as his limbs trembled. Brad began to wonder why he was acting as such while Claire knew there was something mental taking place. While they attended to Dameon's needs, the TV began broadcasting a strange signal. The signal's located was unable to be tracked by the authorities as it was all across the TVs and the internet surrounding all of Detroit. The screen flashed with several images of the orange clouds and photos of the wilderness. The screen flashed once more before settling on an image. The image was a figure sitting. Wearing a worn-out witch hunter hat and a torn coat. the figure raised its head and revealed its face. A beak-like appearance with glowing orange eyes.

"Detroit" The figure spoke. "I see you have witnessed a small dose of my power. For you do not know who I am nor why I'm on your screens. I am the Crow of Death and I am doing this to show you the fear which dwells within your very souls. Now, I send out the word to the Bionic Rage. Wherever you are, I challenge you to a battle of horrors. Come t my horror house and test yourself against the meddling of your mind. Only then, will you discover the way to save the city from its perpetual fears. You have twenty-four hours to make your decision. Or, the city will be succumbed to fear. A fear everlasting. A fear eternal."

The screen flickered, returning to its ordinary broadcast. Claire and Brad began to wonder what to tell Dameon once he regained his senses. From there, four hours had passed before Dameon had awoke. Finding himself in his home, he stumbled to know why. Yelling about the clouds and how they malfunction his limbs. Claire came to him in a rush, calming him as Brad walked over and sat down in front of him. Dameon breathed heavily, asking questions about the clouds and the people. He wondered if they were affected as he, however he learned they were not. He was affected by being in the air while the civilians were on the ground. The clouds never reached the streets and the civilians were spared.

"There's something else." Brad said.

"What's happened now?" Dameon asked. "Vargas is out or is there some new hit man out to get me?"

"Well, someone has come to the city to meet you." Claire said. "But, they're not what you're expecting."

"Tell me who?"

"While you were fighting the effects of the cloud, some stranger sent out a broadcast feed throughout the entire city." Brad answered. "Called himself the Crow of Death and he challenged you to a meet up."

"Meet up where?"

"Dameon." Claire paused. "You can't be serious about confronting this guy. We don't know who is he or why he's doing what he's doing."

"That's the point. You're saying he's responsible for the clouds? Therefore, he's responsible for malfunctioning my limbs and sending my mind into a terrified state."

"Terrified how?" Brad wondered. "You kept going on about dead soldiers and incoming missiles. What did you see?"

"I saw the war before the all the heroes rose. The Republic War. The war that is responsible for my current condition."

"I was there, remember." Brad smiled.

"It seems those memories still have a trigger on you." Claire noted. "I thought you overcame them."

"It's not so simple. Anyway, I will confront this Deathcrow and let him know how I operate."

"But, he didn't give a place exactly." Claire said.

"He did say something about a horror house." Brad pointed out. "I'm not sure what that means or where it is."

Dameon took a moment to think. He stood up, keeping his balance. Claire and Brad rose up to help him, yet he refused. Walking to the workplace in the home, he began prepping his limbs. Fixing the small damage, the clouds caused. The bullets within his forearms were still ready, however he chose to pack several machine gun rounds, wearing them across his chest.

"Where are you going?" Claire asked.

"I'm going to find out where this guy is. Get this over with."

"But, you don't know where he is."

"Yet," Brad said. "Maybe he'll give out a signal. If he truly wants to meet with you, he'll' have something out there for you to see."

"As they all do."

Dameon walked outside and flew into the sky as Claire and Brad watched on.

IV

OVERCOMER

While flying through the air, small flashes of the hallucinations echoed through Dameon's mind. Shaking them off, he returned to downtown Detroit in search of clues. Around him were nothing but civilians who were surprised to see him walking. Others moved away from in fear after seeing him crouched. While he moved, a echo uttered in his ear. A voice unfamiliar to him. Catching onto it, he followed the voice as it led him to a field outside of the city. Once he arrived, Dameon found himself standing in front of an abandoned home. Weather-worn and breaking apart. The home had two floors and Dameon keened his ears and heard the same echo coming from within the home.

"This is the place, huh." Dameon said. "I hope you're ready to see me."

Dameon hovered over the rotten fence surrounding the home. Landing on the concrete pathway heading toward the home's front door, Dameon walked. Stepping closer to the door and once he reached out to open it, the door creaked, opening itself. Dameon scoffed as he entered. Coming into the home, the door closed behind him to where he chuckled. Looking around the home, finding himself standing in the living room area. No electronics were seen, however, there was the remains of old furniture. Rotten and spoiled with liquids unable for Dameon to determine. The home reeked of an odor only found in septic tanks.

"The Bionic Rage." said a voice coming from the balcony above Dameon. "You have come."

"I have. Why don't you show yourself rather than speaking in the dark."

From the shadows of the balcony came forth Deathcrow. Dameon took a small step back and one step forward. Deathcrow's beak glowed with his eyes as he raised up his arms. Dameon lifted up his arms as they cocked. Ready to fire. Deathcrow lowered his arms as the orange clouds began to rise up from the wooden floors.

"I wonder if you're keen to find me in the midst of your fears."

"I've already had a taste of your smoke. I don't perceive it will affect me again."

"We shall see. Let the games begin."

The clouds began to encompass the room as Dameon blasted the nearby doorway with his shotgun rounds. Rushing into the room to avoid the orange clouds, a whiff of the clouds appeared before him from the cracks through the walls, streaking across his face. Brushing it off, he looked around and began to revisit his old memories once more. Seeing more dead soldiers laying throughout the home. Some even called out to him.

"No. it's not real." Dameon reminded himself. "Only a façade. A charade."

"Is it truly a charade?" Deathcrow spoke from within the shadows. "Are you certain your past has not yet been put behind. You walk about as a hero, but are you truly worthy of the claim?"

Dameon went and bolted down several more doors in his path, making way for the clouds to move around within the house. Stepping up the stairs, Dameon caught a glimpse of Deathcrow as he peeked from another room. Dameon ran toward the room, kicking down the door. Inside was darkness. Dameon raised his left hand, unveiling a flashlight within the palm. He entered the room and searched. Only finding a bed and shelves, no sign of Deathcrow.

"The hell did you go?"

"Above and below." Deathcrow replied, standing behind Dameon.

Stomping the floor, Dameon fell back to the first floor inside the living room area. Shaking himself as he arose, Deathcrow walked down the staircase, rating on about Dameon's perceived heroism. Dameon checked his arms, changing the rounds as Deathcrow walked closer.

"I only see a man who wishes to run away from his past. From his failures."

"You know what I see?" Dameon asked. "A fool playing dress up."

Dameon's right arm cocked as he raised it, firing a shot into Deathcrow's chest. death crow fell to the floor, holding the wound in pain as only faint screamed muffled out from his beaked mask. Dameon stood up and stood over him.

"This game is over."

"What are you waiting for?" Deathcrow asked. "Finish me off. Prove to yourself you are not the hero people see you as."

Dameon forwarded his arm, the bullet ready to go. The gears turning within as Deathcrow can hear the chamber in Dameon's arm set to fire. The gears turned and they silenced. Dameon lowered his arm and shrugged his shoulders.

"No need. I've already proven it."

"You are not finished here!" Deathcrow yelled. "The game has only just begun!"

"Tell the police about your game. I won't be tending to it."

Dameon exited the home and flew off. The police came to the home much later and found Deathcrow leaning against the wall, holding his bloody wound. Several days later, Nathan Armstrong came TO Dameon's home. Speaking with him concerning the federal government's watch on him. Nathan warns Dameon they are seeking to obtain hIs bionic limbs and unlike their scuffle with Nathan Hawke and the Nano Man technology, they believe they can achieve the victory over him. Dameon grinned, stating if the government seeks his limbs, they'll have to come and take them.

Later in the day, Dameon went on his casual walk with Brad accompanying him. The two discuss Dameon's plans of being the hero to Detroit. While they talked, three ninjas appeared before them quick as smoke. Dameon removed his coat, showing his bionic arms as they cocked. Brad stood next to Dameon with a glock in his hand.

"Who are you?" Dameon asked.

"What's with the claw marks on your suits?" Brad questioned.

The ninjas moved, striking Dameon and Brad at once. Knocking them down, Dameon arose, blasting gunfire into the air, only to see the ninjas were gone. Brad grabbed his glock from the ground, putting it back to his side. He looked around the area, seeing the ninjas were gone.

"The hell were they?"

"New faces." Dameon said.

"So, I take it they'll be your next objective, huh?"

"Appears that way."

TERROR: WAR ZONE

I

FIRST STRIKE

Meanwhile in Chicago, a group of teenagers are on the run, in fear for their lives. While running through South Chicago, a white van appeared from the street, chasing the teenagers down. While running, one of the teenagers spot an alleyway and yelled for his friends to follow. Rushing toward the alley, the van made a surprising turn, appearing right in between them and the alley. The teenagers paused as two men exited the van and proceeded to drag the teenagers inside. While they began screaming for help, the men slapped them.

"Quit your whining. You could be a valuable asset to our boss."

The two were dressed in all white suits from head to toe. Their eyes shielded by their sunglasses. As one of the men went to put one of the teenagers into the van, a gunshot fired. Startling the men as they looked ahead, seeing John Terror on his motorcycle.

"Shit! He's found us!"

The two men ignored the teenagers and went into the van, pulling out two AKs as they fired toward Terror. Terror swerved the motorcycle and fired several shots from his machine guns. The teenagers ran into the alleyway to avoid the gunfire. Ducking their heads as the bullets echo in the air. They held their heads down as the gunshots continued. Unsure of their lives, the shots silenced as only the dropping of bullets could be heard. The teenagers all looked at one another before taking small steps to the road. Only to find the two men killed and Terror standing over them. They paused themselves out of fear. Terror turned back, seeing the teenagers. They stared.

"Why were they after you?" Terror asked.

"We don't know." One of the teenagers said. "They told us their boss sees us as valuable."

"Valuable how?" Terror asked, looking at the van.

"We don't know."

While checking the van, Terror found a clipboard in the passenger seat. Reading the details and turning the pages, Terror came across the logo for Agency X. he sighed with bitter. Looking at the teenagers, he wondered. However, keeping his thoughts to himself.

"Go ahead and run home. Don't be out in the streets."

"Thank you!" The teenager yelled as they all ran.

Terror ripped the papers from the clipboard and tossed them away. Looking down at the two men's bodies, Terror had an idea.

Sometime later, more Agency X soldiers had arrived, seeing one of their vans sitting at an alley. Coming out from the vehicle was Professor Mite who approached the alley and quickly saw the remaining rounds of bullets on the sidewalk.

"He found them."

With Mite were his two bodyguards, Hunter Vazquez and Mistress Destroyer. They walked toward the alley and found the two men tied up with the torn papers from the clipboard surrounding them. On one piece of paper, Destroyer knelt down and grabbed it from the dead man's hand, handing it to Mite. He read the paper and on it was a warning from Terror to end Agency X for good unless he wanted to face death once more. Mite grinned, balling up the paper and tossing it at the bodies.

"Terror again?" Vazquez questioned.

"As it ever is." Destroyer replied. "We could've killed him if it weren't for his woman and comrade."

"Don't worry yourselves." Mite said. "You shall have your chance once again. For this is an act of war."

"So, what are you proposing we do, Professor?" Vazquez questioned with a grin.

"Go and find Terror and his comrades. Kill them."

"With pleasure." Vazquez replied.

11

RALLY THE UNITS

Terror made his return to his base where Carl Prater waited for him. Walking inside, Terror quickly saw how Prater was looking over a map. Terror approached the table, tossing a torn piece of the notes from the Agency X van. Carl glanced at the paper, seeing the remains of their logo.

"They're still out there?"

"Yeah. This time targeting teenagers."

"Seriously? Ugh. Are we sure we're doing the right thing?"

"What do you mean?" terror asked.

"Doing what we do. Hunting down anything that remains of Agency X across this city. The fact they're just driving around only proves they still have some sense of operation ongoing."

"We took out their base. The job was done."

"But, they're still here. And by what you said regarding the teenagers, that would mean they have another base of operations somewhere nearby."

"And that one will be taken out as well. No problem."

"I take it that's next on your agenda?"

"Always." Terror said, loading up several weapons.

He door to the base had opened, grabbing the attention of Terror and Carl. Looking out as Jade Horror entered the base. Carl let out a sigh of relief, somewhat startled by the sudden arrival of Agency X forces, not to mention Mite's legion of nubreeds. Jade walked over and greeted the two. She looked at the table, seeing the map and the torn paper. The red X on the paper caught her attention much faster than the map itself.

"Them again?"

"Yeah." Terror answered. "I'm about to head out and see where they're operating."

"You know the place?"

"I do not. That is why I'm going out."

"Just like that? You're going to go out there and expect to run into the place where they might be?"

Terror looked over to Carl. He shrugged his shoulders.

"Yeah."

Jade sighed in annoyance at Terror's decision. She walked over to the table and began asking Carl about the markings on the map. Informing her of other possible bases for Agency X. She continued on with more questions while Terror walked over to the refrigerator and took out a bottle of water. He sat down facing them and just observed.

"What about this spot?" Jade asked.

"We've done some scouting around it." Carl answered. "No sign of them there."

"Ok. Then, what of this one?"

"Same conclusion as the first."

Terror shook his head, taking a sip while watching.

Elsewhere, Jordan Dodson went throughout Chicago searching for any information that may track down Agency X. doing the work in favor of Terror's cause, she began researching possible location which were used as scientific facilities near or outside the city limits. Jordan traveled through many of the districts within the city. Upon one stop, she noticed two motorcycles in the distance behind her. The men were in suits and sunglasses. Clad in black. One had a goatee. The other did not. Jordan continued her work and the men followed.

Back at the base, Jordan and Carl came to a concluded stop. Jade marked the location on the map as Terror stood up and approached. He glared down at the mark, seeing the location.

"You've checked there yet?" Jade asked.

"Why would I?" Terror answered. "The place is a nightclub for the heathens. No way Mite would have operations running through there. His team isn't as silent, remember."

"Well, perhaps we should go and check out the place."

"A nightclub?"

"Yeah. What's the worse that could happen?"

Terror sighed.

"Oh, John I figured something out."

"What have you found?"

"Those teenagers you saved… I discovered some more information. Thanks to Jordan, of course."

"She's proven useful." Terror said. "What did she send you?"

"Those teenagers were doing some business with Scarface."

"Scarface?" Jade said. "Who the hell is Scarface?"

"He's a criminal. Not exactly one of the prime bosses of the city, but he's powerful to an extent."

"So, we should interrogate this Scarface guy before we head on out to the club."

"No need." Terror said.

"Why?"

"Scarface runs the club."

Terror grabbed the rest of his gear. Heading on out with Jade following. While they were away, Carl continued to work on the possible site of Agency X's current operations. Communicating with Jordan as she began to warn him about the two Agents who've been tracking her since she began researching their location. Out of fear, Carl told Jordan to come to the base for safety.

Once the night had come, Terror and Horror entered the nightclub. Seeing the crowded state, Jade began asking where Scarface might be. Terror looked out and pointed toward the wall across from the entrance. She glared, seeing a man stylized in an all-grey suit, sitting with ten women. Even with the lights flickering, Jade looked and saw the noticeable scar across his face.

"Oh! That's why he's called Scarface."

"What else did you expect?" Terror shrugged.

They moved with haste, approaching the booth. Two guards stepped in front of them, only for Terror to take them out with two separate blows to the face. With the rap music beating loudly, the attacks did not alert the dancers nor the bouncers. Scarface looked up as did the women, seeing Terror and Horror staring him down.

"Oh shit. What happened now?"

"He talks like this." Jade said. "I thought he might've been more forceful."

"We have some things to discuss." Terror said.

"What things? What does the infamous John Terror seek to know?"

"I want to know about the teenagers you ratted out to Agency X."

"Oh. That bunch. If that's what you want to know, let us talk outside."

Terror nodded, stepping aside.

"After you."

Scarface shoved the women from him, standing up and walking out toward the exit. Coming outside the club as the music faded, Terror and Horror stepped out behind him. Scarface sighed, taking out a cigar. He looked out toward the streets.

"Why have you come to interrupt my night?"

"The teenagers." Terror said. "Why did you hand them over to Agency X?"

"It wasn't a simple handover. It was a business transaction."

"Smuggling teenagers is far beyond business." Jade bolted.

"I know you think such an action is harsh. Maybe chaotic. But, as you, John, know. I am a businessman, and they came to me with a great proposal."

"A proposal of what?"

"To lure you out."

Within the shadows, lunged Vazquez and Destroyer. The two ambushed Terror and Horror with a sudden surprise. Unable to catch themselves, Vazquez and Destroyer decimated the two nubreeds in front of the small crowd that gathered around. Terror stood up and saw Vazquez clearly. He scoffed.

"Cheap shots now."

"Any chance I get to take you out, I'm going to take it."

"Here's your chance." Terror said, removing his coat. "One-on-One."

III

ONE AGAINST MANY

Destroyer and Jade clashes with one another as Jade had her guns knocked out from their holsters as Destroyer kicked them across the street. Jade flipped up, kicking Destroyer in the jaw before leg-sweeping her to the pavement. Terror and Vazquez pummeled one another with straightforward punches to the face. Vazquez, being bigger in size managed to grab Terror by his side and toss him out into the road.

"I thought you would be tougher than this."

"I still am." Terror said, uppercutting Vazquez.

While the four nubreeds fought, an Agency X van pulled up near the club and out of it came the rest of Mite's soldiers. Ranging from the sharpshooter Kudo Fox, the mercenary Hellshot, and the two agents, 50 and 51. Terror kicked Vazquez in the chest as he looked out, seeing the others coming and Mite leaning against the van. Mite stared down Terror and he done the same. Seeing this as an opportunity, Terror bolted, elbowing Vazquez in the face as he made the run for Mite. Jade gained an upper hand against Destroyer, making sure Destroyer's claws don't make a mark across her skin. While fighting, she gazed over seeing Terror running across the street for Mite.

"John! Don't!"

Terror ignored Jade's yell and kept his eyes on Mite. Blocking him from gaining the opportunity was Hellshot, who tripped Terror to the ground and stomped him. Kudo did the same while tossing in several kicks to Terror's abdomen. Jade went to help, Destroyer latched onto her hair, dragging her down and slashing away with her claws. Mite watched on as Vazquez, Hellshot, and Kudo pummeled error into the road, causing a crack to form from their combined might. Over near the club's entrance, Jade remained on the ground, scratched up by Destroyer. Jade was out for there was too much blood. Terror struggled to stand, Vazquez stomped him in the back and held his weight over him. Terror screamed as he tried to shove Vazquez off. Mite clapped as he approached Terror. Knelling down in front of him.

"Is this what you truly wanted?" Mite asked. "To end up like this? As you always would have."

"You think this will hold me down?"

"No. I know your regenerative cells will overcome the damage you've taken tonight. But, howbeit, this is not the end. The war you began is yet to be finish."

"Maybe you should have thought about that earlier before making deals with some club owner."

"Scarface and I have a shared interest. To expand the Agency X foundation across Chicago. Only with your interferences have we come to a sudden stop. No matter. Once we've dealt with you and your associates, Agency X will have a place in this city and soon in the cities beyond."

Mite arose, commanding his soldiers to stand down. Vazquez removed his foot, only to knock out Terror with a kick to the face. Only hearing the faint sounds of their leave did Terror pass out. Nearly thirty minutes later, Carl arrived at the club, seeing Terror and Jade knocked unconscious near the exit.

"What happened?" Carl asked.

Getting some assistance from the hesitant club bouncers, Carl had Terror and Jade placed in the car. Driving back to the base. Within an hour, Terror was awake and healed from the wounds suffered. Looking over at the opposite table, Terror saw Jade awake, but still in some minor pain.

"You live." Jade said.

"The same could be said of you. Your cuts are healed."

"Healing factor does come in handy."

"I can say the same." Terror grinned.

"You never told me how you inherited it." Jade wondered. "Like, were you born with it, or did they give it to you?"

"Another time." Terror said, sensing something from the outside. "Right now, we have to prepare."

Jordan entered the base with a dread of fear pouring from her countenance. Carl rushed to her aid, asking her questions about her hesitancy to enter. She pointed to the outside and Carl went to look at the behest of Terror, who was already getting dressed. Jade began doing the same, yet much slower. Carl peeked outside at the door and saw the two motorcycles parked across the street and the two agents making their way toward the door.

"Shit!" Carl said. "They've found us!"

IV

THE WAR OF CHICAGO

The doors blasted open with a quick and sudden boom. Blasting Terror, Jade, Carl, and Jordan back several feet and destroying the front interior of the base, the two Agents rushed in with open fire. Everyone ducked as the bullets flew over them. Terror shook his head in anger and looked over to Jade. Her emerald eyes showed her intensions and Terror loved it. The two ran over to the closet, taking out weapons ranging from pistols and machine guns. They turned back, returning fire. The Agents leaned against the walls, avoiding the quickening rounds.

"What about us?!" Carl asked.

"Get up and grab a weapon!" Terror answered. "You know the rest!"

While the shootout continued, at the door entered Mite, Vazquez, Destroyer, Kudo, and Hellshot. Mite moved his head to the side, avoiding a speeding bullet. Vazquez sniffed the base, as the air was filled with gun smoke.

"This is what I'm talking about!"

"You know what to do." Mite said, pointing outward, commanding them to strike.

Mite's soldiers rushed into the battle in the midst of the gunfire. Terror looked, seeing Vazquez lunging toward them across the wall. Jade saw Destroyer making her way toward her. Hellshot and Kudo stood next to the Agents and fired back. Terror glared Vazquez and dropped the machine gun. Terror ran and tackled Vazquez to the ground and the two began their pummeling scuffle. Jade watched on as Destroyer interrupted her, swiping the pistol from her hand and twirling her arms as the claws ejected.

"Not again." Jade said, ducking down under the claws.

Carl and Jordan took their shots against the two Agents, Hellshot, and Kudo. Jordan peeked and fired a shot, hitting Hellshot in the knee. His sudden reaction caused his finger to pull the trigger, shooting Kudo and the two Agents in their legs. They fell to one knee, holding the wounds in pain.

"The hell was that?!" Hellshot said.

"We could say the same, dipshit!" Kudo replied.

"Don't mind it! It was an accident!"

"Didn't seem like one!" Agent 51 said. "You could've killed us!"

"You're not dead, are you? So, quit your bickering."

"Enough of your childish talk!" Mite yelled. "Eliminate the targets!"

Terror and Vazquez continued their brawl, eventually taking the fight to the outside as Vazquez speared Terror through the wall. Mite followed them, somewhat giving up on the others inside. Jade and Destroyer continued fighting until Jade gabbed the pistol and shot Destroyer in the forehead. Destroyer fell to the floor as Carl and Jordan rushed to Jade's aid.

"Is she dead?" Carl asked."

"Don't think so." Jade answered. "They're not as simple as that."

Out in the streets, Terror and Vazquez punched each other. Kicked one another and tackled each other to the ground. Fighting in the mixture of wrestling and marital arts. Mite stood outside observing the ongoing brawl. Jade, Carl, and Jordan rushed out to see and Mite turned toward them.

"You've defeated Destroyer?"

"One shot to the head is all it took."

"Is that so?"

Carl watched on as Terror received a punch to the face by Vazquez. Something lingered in Carl's mind, he rushed back inside. Jade turned to see where he went off and she commanded Jordan to follow. Mite stepped forward near Jade.

"Why side with the pawns when you could've been a great soldier under my authority."

"You told John the same. I think I'll take my chances."

"None of you understand the purpose of my work. The work that is planned for all of us. A better world for humanity is the ultimate price for all nubreeds."

"That is the problem. I will not be a slave to the likes of you."

"Slavery is the only option your kind will ever have. No matter the country nor the politics."

"We'll see."

Carl and Jordan made their way back outside. In Carl's hand was a phone and he began yelling about speed dialing Professor Cullen Edge, the leader of the Yonderers for help. Mite's eyes widen and immediately he rallied his soldiers to evacuate. Vazquez swiping Terror across his face with an open palm looked up toward Mite, sensing the fear within him.

"What are you doing, Professor?"

"We need to leave now!"

"What for? We have them right where we want them."

"The Yonderers are coming!"

"Yonderers?" Vazquez said. "Let them come! I've wanted to take them all on! We can win this battle!"

"No, you imbecile! Let's get out of here! If we don't leave, our whole operation will be exposed!"

Vazquez sighed with bitter, getting a kick across Terror's face before making their escape. Hellshot, Kudo, and the Agents each made their way toward the van as Vazquez rushed inside the base, carrying out Destroyer. They all jumped into the van and drove off from the base. Once they were gone, Terror regained himself and approached Carl about the speed dial. Carl shrugged his shoulders and let out a small laugh.

"Nah, wanted to see how they'll react. Didn't expect them to just leave."

Terror grinned with a nod as Carl continued to laugh. Once the area was clear, Terror knew he had work to do on the base. Not wanting the civilians of the city to pass by the area and see the interior. Something he does not desire. Over the next several days, Terror, Jade, Carl, and Jordan each put in their hand to restore the base from the shattered wall, the busted door, and to the interior. Once the base was restored, Terror learned of another force lurking through the city. Hearing that Scarface was in communications with the unseen group, Terror paid him another visit at his club. Only this time he was not ambushed by Mite's soldiers. Terror dragged Scarface to his back office and interrogated him about the group. Terror demanded to know a name.

"Alright! I'll tell you who they are!"

"Better speak now before the wall is covered with your blood."

"Ok. The group, they're the ones who told me about the teenagers in the first place. I just gave Agency X the information regarding them. That's all!"

"Name!" Terror yelled.

"They call themselves the Warriors of the Claw." Scarface said clearly. "That's all I know."

Terror put away his gun and turned away. Scarface sighed as he wiped the sweat from his forehead. Terror from that moment, began his search for the Warriors of the Claw.

Q-ARROW: MINUTES OF ALTER

I

THE FUTURE

The Las Vegas Strip was celebrating a party of some kind. Unsure if it was for an anniversary, someone's birthday, or just a casual party for all. The civilians came and went. All partaking in the party. While the strip was filled with people, both Las Vegas citizens and tourists, a bright flash spread forth from the sky. The light grabbed their attention with haste. All gazing up to the stars, from the light a figure emerged. His appearance awed them. White and blue from his neck down. Standing on a silver disc with was reminiscent of solid platinum.

"Las Vegas!" The man said. "Your savior has come!"

The people looked on at the man as he came to the ground. Smiling and showing a sign of welcome toward them. He began to speak about his appearance. Claiming to be a man from the future. Above him more flashes of light occurred and emitting from them were a dozen men. All wearing the same attire as him. However, they each carried a small handgun and their faces covered in helmets. The people at that point began to take steps back. Although, the stranger began warning them to calm down. He stated the men are with him to find and track Q-Arrow.

"Q-Arrow is not a hero. Regardless of his previous actions! You may think he's a hero. But, he's not! He's a troublemaker and the things he's got planned will turn your party-filled city into nothing but a crater of sand."

The people listened as an arrow pierced into the ground, startling them and the stranger. From above came down Q-Arrow and Shadow

Hardy. The stranger grinned and clapped his hands as his men clenched their handguns, forming a single line besides the stranger. Q-Arrow glanced at the people and turned toward the strangers, seeing his men armed.

"Who are you?"

"A Minuteman. No need to be all mysterious."

"And why have you come?"

"To warn the people of your true nature."

"My true nature being?"

"To destroy Las Vegas."

Q-Arrow looked over toward Hardy, who had nothing to say. He turned back to the people and saw the fear in their eyes. Yet, not for him. He nodded and faced the Minuteman. His fingers tapping on the bow. Hardy stood his ground, monitoring the men around Minuteman.

"I'm not going to destroy the city."

"Oh, you will."

"And how do you know of this?"

"Because, as I told the good people of this city, I'm from the future!"

"The future?" Q-Arrow said.

"Yes! How else could I have known about your actions to come."

"He's bluffing." Hardy said.

"Oh, young man. I'm not lying. If I were, I wouldn't be from the future."

"Then, what do you want?" Q-Arrow asked. "Name something before I make a decision."

"I want you to expose yourself. Tell these people the truth about what you have planned for yourself and this city."

Q-Arrow sighed. He turned around to the people and nodded.

"What I have planned is this. To protect the people of this city at any cost. Even from those seeking to divide us only with cheap words and a ridiculous entrance."

Minuteman clapped his hands while letting out a laugh. The civilians continued to watch on as Q-Arrow gripped his bow tightly, seeing the men behind Minuteman prepared to fire. Hardy moved forward in striking position. Minuteman looked at him and Q-Arrow, nodding with a point.

"Is that what you want?"

"Only when you make the call."

"When I make the call. Very well, Timeguards! Do your thing!"

The Timeguards opened fire. Scattering the civilians as Arrow and Hardy made their moves around the Strip. Arrows fired, knocking several handguns from their hands, giving Hardy a way to bolt in and strike down the guards. Minuteman moved out of the fighting, taking the option to watch from a distance. Although he moved far from them, Q-Arrow kept his eye on him and aimed an arrow, taking the shot. The arrow dented the device which Minuteman stood on. He grinned.

"Nice shot! But, I have to go!"

"Oh, hell no!" Q-Arrow said, firing more arrows.

The arrows went through Minuteman as he became transparent and vanished before their eyes. Even the timeguards vanished. Q-Arrow looked around and Hardy searched the surroundings of the civilians. Arrow looked out toward the rest of Vegas. Lingering in his mind was one question: where did Minuteman go?

II

THE PAST

Returning to the Arrowlair, Asher and Jeff began their discussion regarding Minuteman's sudden arrival alongside his Timeguards. Inside the lair stood by Jarvis Hoyt and Arwin Reese. Asher looked around the lair, seeing much of the new equipment from grappling tech to new arrows. He pointed it out to Jarvis' laughter.

"New upgrades for your outgoing adventures."

"Seems convenient. Where did you get all of this from?"

"From your friend over in Retropolis. Appears he owed you a favor."

"Oh. Appears he did."

"Now, what happened out there?" Arwin asked. "I'm curious."

"We came across a guy who claims to have come from the future."

"The future?" Jarvis said. "And why would he appear in Vegas of all places? For what purpose?"

"He came to warn the people. About me. Said I'm planning their destruction."

"And what future did this guy come from?" Arwin asked. "Because there's nothing here that signals your world domination. Not you of all people. Now, there are some out there who fit the bill for world conquest and Asher, my friend, you are not one of them."

"That's good to know, Arwin. Good to know."

"Now, where is this future guy?" Jarvis questioned. "Is he still in the city or something?"

"He vanished. Right before our eyes. My arrows went through him."

"Through him how?"

"His body became transparent before he vanished."

"Well, you know all of this would be useful if we had some of his tech." Arwin said. "Did he leave any of it out there?"

"I didn't see any." Asher answered. "What about you, Jeff?"

"I got something."

Jeff presented them with one of the timeguards' handguns. Arwin held it and was amazed at its appearance. The carving of the handle was profound in his eyes. To theirs it was only a handgun. Arwin went an examined the material the gun was made of and came to a surprising conclusion. After an hour, he presented to them the information he learned. The gun is made from an element not yet discovered.

"So, they are from the future." Asher said. "Just great."

"What element is it made of?" Jarvis asked. "Because I can send word around. Figure something out."

"Unless you know someone who works in nanotechnology, I can't help you."

"Very well." Asher said. "Contact our friend up north. Tell him to send the data to Nathan Hawke. He will learn more about this tech."

"Nathan Hawke?" Arwin said. "You're talking about the Hawke Industries guy?"

"Yeah."

"How would he be of help?"

"Because he works in nanotechnology."

"Oh." Arwin said. "Wasn't aware. That's good though."

"Are you going to rest up and catch this guy tomorrow?" Jarvis asked.

"No. I need to find him tonight." Asher answered. "The night is still young after all."

"True words spoken."

While Arwin and Jarvis worked on equipping some of Asher's gear with a small fragment from the futuristic gun, Asher and Jeff trained. Remembering their previous encounters with the Dominate Trio, Woodstalker, Rattler, Eaglestruck, Komodo Dragon, and Hitman. While training, Jeff questioned why Asher chose the path of a hero. Asher paused himself from his boxing session.

"You've seen Vegas just as I have. There aren't any other heroes here."

"But, if there were, would you still continue on as the Q-Arrow?"

"Of course, I would."

"Why?"

"Because of a promise I made."

"A promise? Who'd you promise?"

"Myself."

Jeff could only nod. While they finished their training, Jarvis approached Asher with his bow. Holding it, Asher looked closer as the bow began to glow in the similar fashion as the gun. Asher nodded with interest. Twirling the bow and taking it into the practice room. Firing the new arrows against the targets. To his amazement, the new arrows were Kevlar-laced. capable of piercing through armored enemies.

"He knew exactly what I needed."

"I take it you're about to head back out there and find this Minuteman?"

"What other choice do I have."

"While you were sparring, Karen called. Said she wants to speak with you tomorrow concerning some business matters."

"Sure. Jeff, you ready?"

"Yes sir."

Asher walked into his changing room and donned the Q-Arrow gear, heading on out with his motorcycle as Hardy followed on his own.

III

THE PRESENT

Q-Arrow and Shadow Hardy made their return to the Strip. Appearing at the same location. Arrow began calling out Minuteman, commanding him to show up out of the darkness and face him. Right above them, the bright light flickered, and Minuteman appeared with this time guards. Minuteman grinned seeing Q-Arrow and even gave him an applause as he came down.

"You called out to me. I'm touched."

"This ends tonight. All of it."

"But, we just met did we not? You can't rush something like this."

"Oh, I am. Trust me."

Arrow extended his bow. Hardy was prepped for the fight as were the time guards. Minuteman stood in anger. The timeguards held up their guns. Ready to aim whenever Minuteman commanded them. Arrow grinned, firing the arrow across the guards, swiping the guns from their hands and exploding them to Minuteman's surprise.

"Didn't see that coming did you."

"Come on man! No one-ups!"

The timeguards were then unsure how to attack. Quickly, Arrow signaled Hardy for the attack, taking out the guards in a matter of seconds with his swift speed. Minuteman watched on as his men were eliminated. Turning toward Q-Arrow, who had an arrow aimed for his head.

"You're going to just kill me? Like that?"

"I'm not that kind of hero."

"Don't lie to me." Minuteman pointed. "As I told you prior, I know your future. I've seen what you become and what you do."

"Then you come from another future. The future I have planned does not include the deaths of many nor does it include my betrayal."

"How would you know of your future? You haven't lived it yet. I have."

The arrow pulled back. Minuteman held his hands up with a smile. Arrow did not laugh. No emotion could be pulled from his face and Minuteman knew this. Hardy remained in position.

"What's the problem? Take the shot. Finish me off."

"No. I'm not going to kill you. I'm warning you."

"Of what?"

"You return to this city, this time, I will not hesitate to take you out."

Minuteman chuckled and clapped some more. He began to savor the moment. Taking one step further as Arrow cleaned the bow with the sound of the band stretching. Minuteman stopped and held his hands up.

"Very well. You want me gone? I get it. But, I cannot assure you that I will keep your word."

"Don't and see what ends up with your future."

"I like a good challenge. Alright then, Golden Archer, I'll be seeing you around. Keep watch!"

Minuteman clapped his hands, pulling out a controller of some kind from his pocket. Pressing the button, several white holes which resembled black holes had appeared with wind-like gusts. They carried with them a pressure of their own. The wind could be heard, but not felt. the timeguards vanished into sudden white hole portals. Q-Arrow was amazed at the tech and kept his focus on Minuteman. His arrow was still pulled back on the bow. Set to fire whenever Q-Arrow deemed it. Even the guns of the timeguards were sucked in. Tipping over into the portals and vanishing into the bright light. Minuteman saluted Arrow as he entered the final portal, yelling of his impending return. The portals closed and silence remained. This time no civilians were nearby to witness the small event. Q-Arrow turned to Hardy and sighed.

"This is not over."

"What's next?" Hardy asked. "We track him down?"

"We keep this city protected. That's what's next."

KULAR THE AQUA-BARBARIAN: SEAS OF WAR

I

PREPARATION

The Kingdom of Atlantis is moving with sheer force. A nonstop motive to prepare for war against the other forces throughout the seas. After Kular's clash with Lord Shark, the discovery of the Sea-Stormers' return proved enough fro the King of Atlantis to make the decision to prepare. All warriors were ready and at arms. Guarding the entrance into the kingdom. Staring out into the open sea, no sign of life like their own could be seen. Only the fish of the sea.

Currently inside the palace, Kular sat alone, waiting for the moment the first enemy came to the kingdom's gates. Sitting in his study, meditating on the battle to come. Hearing a knock from the door, he permitted the visitor to enter. Coming through the door was Kular's advisor, Novah. Novah went and show obeisance to the king before speaking what was on his mind.

"I see the soldiers are prepared for the coming conflict." Novah said.

"As they should be. As we all should be."

"No worries, my king. We've dealt with much worse events in times prior. Prior before the heroes of the surface made themselves known."

"I often wonder. If I do the surface world a favor by aligning myself with their heroes, won't it be so in times to come, they'll come and aid us in our favor."

Novah chuckled, sitting at the table across from Kular.

“I’ve yet to meet these heroes the surface world clearly praise. However, you have. From what you’ve told us, they’re a powerful force. All coming with their own abilities and each proven for the use they provide. Now, you tell me. Are any of them trustworthy to aid us in our cause against the incoming armies?”

“Yes.” Kular said. “Without question. As far as I know there are a few.”

“What if we sent out word to the surface world. See which of these heroes you’ve encountered come to aid us.”

Kular’s eyes widen as he sat back in his seat. Thinking on the topic. He nodded.

“Do what you can. Hopefully the ones I’ve met will find a way to come down and help us. I know in their heart they’ll do whatever it takes to defeat such forces.”

Novah stood up and bowed before Kular as he took his leave from the study. Entering after him was Kara as she walked over and kissed Kular. Kular took a moment to observe Kara’s attire. The long pink dress which flowed with the waves of the sea.

“Why have you come to see me?” Kular smiled.

“You weren’t anywhere else. I figured you would be in here studying or mediating. Seems you were doing he latter. Aside from your talk with Novah.”

“He’s only making sure I’m ready for what’s coming to us all.”

“And what do you think is coming for us aside from the armies of the seas?”

“Who knows. Novah did give me some great insight.”

“Him being your advisor, it is his job to give you great insight. Plus, his advice has helped you come a long way.”

“That is true.” Kular said. “He did however bring up a good idea.”

“What kind of idea?”

“That we send out word to the surface world. To the heroes. See if they’ll aid us in our war.”

“And you think they will?”

“Some will. That I know for certain.”

Kular held Kara close as he looked out toward the open sea to the light which shined into the waters slowly faded into the night.

II

THE FIRST CONFLICT

The morning had come over Atlantis. The soldiers remained at their post. Looking outward. Over in the distance ahead of the city, the watchmen gazed out, seeing a moving force coming toward the kingdom. Getting a better look with their scopes, they saw an army. Nearly sixty soldiers and leading them was an armored individual. Clad in a molten black. His face shielded by his helmet which gave off a lava-red glare.

"Intruders!" The watchman yelled. "Intruders are here!"

Kular, Kara, and Novah rushed outside to see the army. Novah knew them well. Pointing out the leader's armored appearance.

"You know who they are?" Kular asked.

"I do. They're tee Manta Clan. Their leader is called the Manta Master."

"Fetch your best weapon, Novah. We'll need every hand on deck for this one."

"Right away."

"I'm fighting too." Kara said.

"I'm not certain that's a good idea."

"You said you need every hand. I can handle myself. Why else would I be training for?"

Kular agreed with hesitance. Looking out toward the Manta Kingdom's coming arrival. He commanded Kara to grab her best weapon and prepare for the fight. Kara smiled, rushing back inside the place. Kular held his trident and slammed it into the ground, making his way toward the front with his soldiers. The soldiers looked and greeted their king. Delighted of him to join them.

"Are you all ready?" Kular asked.

"We are!" The soldiers responded.

"We can take them. As we've dealt with the others who have come and done the same. For this is Atlantis! Our home!"

The soldiers hyped themselves by chanting, 'Victory for Atlantis!'. Kular stood front and center as the Manta Kingdom sped themselves up and bolted toward the kingdom. The gates closed behind the soldiers as they stepped forward. Walking past the gate before it closed were Novah and Kara. Each equipped with their own weapon. Novah carried a scythe while Kara held a trident of her own with five points aside from Kular's three-pointed one.

"What of the call?" Kular questioned Novah. "Did you send one out?"

"Before nightfall. Word went out. Hopefully one of your surface friends will come and aid us."

"We can only hope."

The Manta Kingdom inched closer as their leader paused, holding up a spear of his own. Glowing like magma under the waters. He held it up and aimed it toward the kingdom. His soldiers screamed and all ran with an increased speed toward the Atlanteans. Kular rallied up his soldiers once more as they ran toward the Manta soldiers. All clashing into one another with swords, spears, and tridents. The Manta Master stepped aside while swiping incoming Atlantean soldiers from his path. His glare was focused on Kular and the Aqua-Barbarian's eyes were the same. Within the fight, Kara and Novah stood together taking over several Manta soldiers who've come into their crosshairs. Kara moved with speed, a speed in which the Manta soldiers could not keep up with. With the use of her trident, twirling the weapon through the fight, tripping and knocking the Manta soldiers down. Novah walked through the fight, swinging his scythe as he sliced off the legs and arms of Manta soldiers.

"Where is Kular's surface friends?" Novah asked. "They could be useful right about now."

Kular fought his way toward the Manta Master. His eyes set on him as he swung his trident across his path, taking out the Manta soldiers in his way. The Manta master laughed as he watched.

"Why have you come?" Kular asked.

"Lord Shark informed all the kingdoms under the seas about your rule. He claimed you were soft. A perfect target for any of us to take out. If you were to fall, the kingdom would be given over to the conqueror. I am that conqueror."

"Only way to make it so is to kill me." Kular said, twirling the trident. "Are you ready for the fight?"

"It's why I'm here."

Manta Master went to spear Kular, yet the trident was in its path. Kular kicked back, stumbling Manta Master for Kular to get in several blows with his trident. The two continued clashing their weapons against each other. Causing small rifts in the air to the point of being seen on top of the water. Kara and Novah continued to go in against the Manta soldiers. The Manta soldiers took a moment ot pause and in a collaborative effort, they all let out a screeching howl. The howl had pierced the waters and even caused Kara, Novah, Kular, and the Atlantean soldiers to cover their eyes from the pressure. Manta Master took the opportunity and swiped his spear against Kular, slamming him into one of the coral posts near the gate. The Manta soldiers continued their screech as Manta Master went ahead and continued to attack Kular on the ground.

"This is how your end is done." Manta Master said.

Kular went to raise up the trident and before Manta Master could make his attack, a beam struck from above, knocking Manta Master back as he dropped his spear. The beam took everyone on the battlefield by surprise. Kular noticed it too well, gazing up and from above like a lightning bolt came down the Nano Man. Kular stood up as the Nano Man turned to him.

"I received a call. Saw it came from under the sea. A challenge worth taking."

Manta Master arose, staring down Nano Man. Calling back his spear. Kara and Novah saw Nano Man standing beside Kular. While everyone gazed at the Nano Man, Kular noticed a distinctive change in Nano Man's armor.

"I see it is of a different color and appearance."

"Surface dweller!" Manta Master screamed, setting up to throw his spear.

Nano Man turned to him and fired another beam against Manta Master, slamming him back to the ground as his spear fell from his hands.

"It's my Hydro Armor. Figured I would be diving into the sea eventually. Just prepared."

"So, you received the call. Are you the only one?"

"Yeah. The others were busy with some circumstances going on up there. Let me guess, you were expecting the sorcerer guy to show up or the young electric fellow?"

"Something of a kind. However, you received the call. Therefore, I will accept your support."

Nano Man nodded, turning back to the risen Manta Master and his army. Nano Man pointed toward them, looking out at the army.

"I take it this is the enemy of the day?"

"It is. Manta Master and his army. They're from the Manta Kingdom."

"Sounds easy to remember. A kingdom of manta-like people. Noteworthy."

"You align yourself with surface-dwellers?" Manta Master asked. "You have forsaken the ancient laws of the seas. Never side with those from above. They only want to seek what we have. Our resources and plunder them for themselves."

"I was once one of those guys." Nano Man said. "Now, I'm just a hero looking to do good. So, I'll start with ridding you guys from this man's kingdom."

Nano Man blasted Manta Master again as Kular yelled for his army to fight back. The battle continued as Kular and Nano Man dealt with Manta Master and on the other side of them the armies clashed. Blood moving through the water as the fight went on. Nano Man blasted several of Manta Master's soldiers before getting rammed by Master's spear. Kular jumped into the gaze of Manta Master and tossed his trident, spearing Master into the coral post. Manta Master used his strength to pull himself from the trident's hold, however his strength was no match for the tug between the trident and the coral. The more he pulled, the deeper the coral took in the trident.

“What is this?” Manta Master questioned as he struggled.

“You’re fighting against the coral.” Kular replied. “If you stop, it may let you go.”

Manta Master continued his struggle as his army was being overtaken by the Atleanteans. With Nano Man’s sudden arrival and the rallying cry from Kular, the Atlanteans increased their vigor and defeated the Manta soldiers. Leaving their master remaining. While he continued struggling to get himself free from the coral, Kular approached him. Standing by his side were Kara, Novah, and Nano Man.

“Do we have terms?” Manta Master asked.

“We have terms.” Kular answered. “Do you surrender?”

“Does it look like I have a choice now.”

Kular grabbed his trident and with a slow pull did he free Manta Master from the coral. Falling to his knees, Nano Man charged up his power as his fingertips began to glow. Kular held his hand up toward Nano Man and the energy ceased. He knew Manta Master was defeated. In Kular’s ruling way, he gave Manta Master and the remaining members of his army leave and they did. Carrying with them their own dead. Once they were away from the kingdom, all Atlanteans celebrated victory. Meanwhile, Kular stood inside his study with Novah and Nano Man.

“Is this one of those surface dwellers you aligned with on your explorations?”

“Not exactly.” Kular answered. “We came into contact by other means.”

“We shared a scrap here and there.” Nano Man said. “All for a good cause.”

Novah nodded while taking the measure of the Nano Man. Kular began overlooking a map of the seas and marked the Manta Kingdom with an X. turning to the next one, which he believed would be the Night-Dwellers. Novah however informed him that would not be the case, since they’ve been missing since the end of the Republic War. Once their discussion was over, Nano Man received a distress call coming from Newark and bid his farewell. Taking off back to the surface.

“One down.” Novah said. “A few more to go.”

“This war is far from over.” Kular said, gazing over map. “I can feel it."

III

THE UNSEEN FORCE

The following day, several of the Atlantean soldiers moved with haste toward the gate. Feeling uneasy, Novah took the moment to gaze out into the open and what he saw quickened him. Rushing toward the study where Kular and Kara were overlooking the map. He burst through the door.

"He's coming."

"Who's coming?" Kara asked.

"The Cuttlefish."

Kular heard the name and rose up from the desk. Grabbing his trident by the door, the three exited and went toward the front gate. Looking out amongst the soldiers, Kular saw the Cuttlefish. Swimming toward them in his human/fish hybrid state. Kara was somewhat confused. She asked why the intruder was called the Cuttlefish. To Novah's surprise, he was dismayed by her ignorance toward the creature. The Cuttlefish screeched with a loud roar, from there rushing into the Atlantean army, shattering their defenses and breaking apart the shields they held. The Cuttlefish even grabbed some of their spears and impaled several soldiers into the coral. Kular rallied for the remaining forces to arrive and coming in with such an increasing force, the Cuttlefish stared. No emotion. Nothingness could be seen on his face, yet its eyes were glaring destruction. Kular, Kara, and Novah ran together and clashed with the sea beast. Its strength was unable to be matched, showing them past the soldiers and through the gate to the kingdom. Kular shook the pain from his back, holding tightly to his trident as Cuttlefish swiped the weapon from Kara's hand. Moving back from the Cuttlefish's nearing attack, Novah leaped into the air and impaled the Cuttlefish in its back as Kular dove straightforward into the Cuttlefish's chest. Kara retrieved her weapons and followed Kular's motive, stabbing the Cuttlefish in the abdomen.

"That should do it." Novah said, holding his own.

The Cuttlefish struggled against the combined efforts of Kular, Novah, and Kara as their weapons were all impaled into its body. From within a moment, the Cuttlefish exhaled and fell into the sand as its body deflated. Kular sighed as he pulled the trident from its body. The remaining soldiers cheered the victory to Kular's tiredness and soreness of body. Once nightfall had touched the sea, Kular sat in his chamber as Kara walked over toward him, seeing the bruises on his chest and back.

"You're never been this damaged before."

"I have. Sometime ago. It's nothing. I'll live."

"So, what now?" Kara said, sitting next to Kular.

"Now, we wait for the Sea-Stormers to arrive. Along with Sea Kaiser."

"I'm not certain he's still alive after your last battle. You killed him right where our gates stand. Truly, he cannot have lived."

"Tomorrow will tell. Right now, I need rest."

IV

I HAVE RETURNED

The next day, Kular, Kara, and Novah were quickly gathered to the outside. Staring out in the distance as they've done the past three days. The Atlantean soldiers took their positions as prior, this time all soldiers carried spears and shields. Novah held his binoculars and looked out into the open. Seeing what was coming, he immediately handed the binoculars to Kular and pointed.

"They're here." Novah said quietly.

Kular looked out and saw the Sea-Stormers. They marched with purpose as the sand kicked up beneath their feet. In front of them was no one. No leader? Kular questioned the uncertain appearance of the Stormers. For they've always had their leader in front no matter the circumstance or location. Kular lowered the binoculars and stared.

"Something's different."

"Different like what?" Kara questioned. "The Stormers are coming. What must we do?"

"They have no leader." Kular said. "No one leads them here. They're moving on their own accord."

"Such an act is unnatural to the laws of the seas." Novah mentioned. "We must question their purpose once they reach the gates."

The Stormers had reached the gates and stood calm. Collected. No expression on their face aside from it being hidden by their helmets. Kular and Novah walked toward them past the gate as the soldiers remained behind them with their spears pointed forward. Kular took the measure of them.

"Where's your leader?"

"He is here." One Stormer said. "Right among you."

"Among us?" Novah questioned. "Point him out!"

The Stormers pointed toward Kular. Standing back as Novah turned to him. Kular raised up his trident and aimed it toward the Stormer.

"I am not your leader!"

"But, you are." The Stormer said. "However, under new orders we have arrived to Atlantis on our master's current call."

"I am not your master. Nor did I call you here."

"I speak of him." the Stormer said, looking upward.

Everyone gazed up and above them was the Sea-Kaiser in full form. His appearance no different than the last encounter between the two kings. The Stormers chanted his name as he took in their reverence. Turning toward Kular and Novah, he grinned.

"You're supposed to be dead." Kular said. "I impaled you."

"Nature has its way of changing the dynamic of reality. Do not worry yourselves, I am not here to fight. I came here as a warning."

"A warning of what?" Novah questioned. "You seek to threaten the king of Atlantis and his kingdom?"

"No. I come to tell you Atlantis will be mine. One day. However, today is not that day."

Sea-Kaiser commanded the Stormers to turn back and retreat the kingdom. As they obeyed, Kular stepped forward, slamming his trident into the sands, causing a great lightning storm to form above them within the waters. Sea-Kaiser paused himself, glaring up at the beautiful sight. He nodded in Kular's show of power.

"You're just going to walk away? After the words spread of your imminent return?"

"Yes." Sea-Kaiser said. "Consider it mercy."

He turned and left with his army. Kular remained as he watched while Novah commanded the army to return inside the gates. The days of war were over.

Following the days after, one of the Atlantean soldiers sought an audience with Kular. Being granted the request, he met with the Aqua-Barbarian and informed him of a disturbance in the waters. Kular questioned the mystery with only the soldier discovering a tool from the surface world. A blade layered with kinetic energy.

"What such a weapon is this?" Novah asked.

"I've seen similar weapons on the surface." Kular answered. "Yet, not one like this."

"What are those markings on the handle?"

Kular looked, seeing the markings. His eyes squinted.

"Looks like claw marks."

"They are." Kular said.

"So, what's next, my king?"

"We prepare for Sea-Kaiser's return. We'll keep hold of this weapon in case enemies of the surface seek to enters our domain."

Novah bowed before exiting the throne room and Kular remained alone. Sitting with only his thoughts and the blade sparking with energy.

ENFORCEMENT ORDER 66: A NEW STRATEGY

I

FIRST CONFLICT

Gunbaine, Hark, Swan, and the others of the Enforcement Order all looked ahead as the Exchange Force made their way toward them. Gunbaine loaded up his weapons and stood up before Hark grabbed him by his shoulder.

"Get off."

"That's suicide. We need to think of something else."

"Like what?" Maria wondered. "We could just go in there blazing. It's only five of them."

"They already know we're here!" Gunbaine said. "We have no other choice."

Hark nodded.

"You're right. Let's finish this."

11

CENTER STAGE

The Enforcement Order all stood up from their hiding place and began firing at the Exchange Force. The mercenary unit moved aside from the incoming blasts as they loaded up their own rounds in retaliation. Gunbaine and Hark stood in front, shooting nonstop as Maria, Black Mare, and G-Zero used their own keenness to distract the members of the Force into the open. Thunderstorm looked up, seeing no clouds. He turned toward Gunbaine and Hark.

"I have an idea."

"Whatever you have in mind, do it." Hark said.

"What he said." Gunbaine replied. "At least give us some cover."

Thunderstorm hovered into the air as the skies began to darken. The Force looked up, seeing the clouds forming above them with streaks of lightning. They each watched on, seeing Thunderstorm in the air with his arms stretched out as lighting struck from his hands and into the clouds. The sun continued to be covered by the dark clouds as rain fell onto the battlefield.

"Give them some strikes while you're at it!" Gunbaine yelled.

Thunderstorm's eyes were shielded by lightning as he commanded the bolts to crash in front of the Force. Blocking them from getting any closer to the team. The Force fired back with their own weapons in the form of grenade and rocket launchers. The explosions from the launchers were able to scatter. Gunbaine and Hark remained in the front, Maria went ahead and stepped forward, yet another attack from a grenade crashed in front of her, blasting her further from the two leaders. Black Mare and G-Zero were down with minor injuries. Thunderstorm continued bolting down lighting in front of the Force.

"We need to get that one down." The female Force member said.

"No problem." The brute Force member replied.

Raising up the rocket launcher and firing without notice, the rocket caught Thunderstorm off his guard, striking him down from the air. As he fell, the sky began to lighten up and the sun peaked in front the dispersing clouds. Gunbaine and Hark looked back, seeing most of their team was down. Hark shook his head and Gunbaine knew they had no chance. Not taking a loss, Gunbaine rushed forward and blasted all five members of the Force with all his weapons. With them fully loaded, Gunbaine took the shots and never blinked. Meanwhile, Hark ran toward his teammates and helped them up. Looking out into the streets behind them, they saw the Moroccan military driving up.

"Shit." Hark turned back to Gunbaine. "Smalls! We need to get out of here!"

"Not with these assholes still walking!" Gunbaine yelled, still firing at the Force.

"Leave them be! We need to go!"

Gunbaine sighed heavily before firing one large blast into the street, which exploded in front of the Force. seeing the explosion, Gunbaine and the rest of the team made their escape from the streets as the military rushed into the shielded street of smoke wittier weapons up. Finding their escape, they made a run for their plane and boarded immediately. Once the plane lifted and took off, Hark received a call from A.B., commanding the team to return to Base 33 for an urgent matter. Hark informed the team of A.B.'s news and could only question why would it be an urgent concern after what they've just went through.

III

A NEW TARGET

Making their return to Base 33, Black Mare, G-Zero, Thunderstorm, and Maria Swan were taken into the medical facility to be rehabilitated. Meanwhile, Gunbaine and Hark walked with the Base 33 guards into A.B.'s office. As the doors opened, hey were completely at a stop, seeing not only A.B. in the office, but another individual. A guest in her words. Gunbaine moved steady as Hark seemed to be afraid.

"Don't go for your weapon, Gunbaine." A.B. said. "You know it won't end well."

"Fair enough. Why is he here?"

A.B. turned around to her desk as the guest in her office was The Swordman. Gunbaine removed his helmet as Hark took a seat near the bookshelf, but he was afraid and The Swordman knew it. The Swordman remained silent, yet his eyes could be felt glaring across the office.

"Take a seat, Smalls." A.B. said.

Gunbaine nodded, taking a seat across from Hark, staring a hole through The Swordman.

"You know our last encounter was a failed state." Gunbaine said toward The Swordman."

"I'm not here for that." Swordman answered. "I'm here for a simple reason. One your boss is aware of."

"And what does my boss know that we don't?" Hark questioned. "Why are you even here in the first place?"

"Better she tell you."

"He wants me to end the Order. To end the team."

"But, we're doing good work here." Hark answered. "Work that can help others across the world. What have you done?"

"Saved the world from an invading force." The Swordman answered. "I have my purpose. You have yours."

A beeping sound emitted from The Swordman's forearm. Glancing down and reading. Without saying a word, he stood up and sheathed his sword, walking toward the exit. Gunbaine stood up.

"That's it? You're just going to go and leave? Like that?"

"Adrian Brown." The Swordman said. "If your team is not disbanded before my next mission is complete, myself and my team will end it for you."

"I'll do what I mist." A.B. replied.

The Swordman took his leave from the office as Hark rushed over toward A.B. Checking to see if she's injured. She shoved him back, showing she was well. Gunbaine continued looking out as he saw The Swordman leaving.

"How did he get in here? I thought this base was heavily secured."

"He has his ways." A.B. said.

"You're not taking his word are you?" Hark questioned. "You're not ending the team?"

A.B. grinned.

"No. I'm not."

"Alright, we need to track down those Force members and finish what we started." Gunbaine said. "Are you ready?"

"Ready when you are." Hark answered.

"Hold on." A.B. said. "That is no longer your mission."

"Then, what is our mission?" Hark said.

"You heard The Swordman. His team will stop us. Let them try."

"You're saying our next mission is facing The Resistance?" Hark asked. "You know who they have?"

"I do and it will prove which team is the strongest. Prepare yourselves gentlemen for the battle of your lives."

UNDERWORLD
A DARK TITAN UNIVERSE EVENT

I

THE DEVIL-KNIGHT

During a crowded night in the Chicago nightclub operated by Scarface. Scarface himself had a meeting in the basement area of the club. His guests were the ninjas with the clawed insignia imbued on their attire. Scarface began to speak to them concerning their plans for the city. During their discussion, the door bolted open as two bouncers fell out. Walking out from the door was the Devil-Knight. The ninjas rallied themselves, taking out their swords. The Devil-Knight smirked as he was only focused on Scarface.

"What do you want?" Scarface asked.

"I want to know where their leader is. Figured you would know. You're speaking with them."

The ninjas looked toward Scarface as he stood there with only a sense of confusion. His eyes going back and forth between Devil-Knight and the ninjas, he yelled for them to attack as he made his escape. Devil-Knight grinned as he rushed into the fight against the ninjas. Holding his own and deflecting their kicks and chops with his forearms. Up above, Scarface bolted through the door, bumping into the guests of the club. Panting for air, he reached toward the front door only to find himself staring at John Terror.

"Oh shit."

"You didn't think I forgot about you?" Terror grinned.

The basement door blew off the hinges as one of the ninjas' bodies flew across the club, landing on the floor next to Scarface. Terror glanced down, seeing the ninja. His focus rose up to Scarface.

"What's happening here?"

"There's a guy down there. He came out of nowhere. The… the ninjas were taking care of him."

"Doesn't look like it's in their favor. Who's the muscle?"

"I don't know."

At the basement door another ninja is tossed out. The guests look toward the door, waiting to see who's coming next and stepping out of the door was Devil-Knight. His glare caused a striking fear to crawl down their spines as they ran out of the club. Terror watched on as the people fled around him. No expression on his face as his eyes are shielded by his sunglasses. Scarface dodged the coming crowd, jumping over the bar and hid. Terror watched as Devil-Knight defeated the remaining ninjas within a few minutes. Once the last ninja was taken down by Devil-Knight's swift haymaker to the back of the head, Terror walked toward him with his arms down. Devil-Knight glared up, seeing Terror standing before him.

"We've never met." Terror said.

"No. but, tonight's the night." Devil-Knight replied. "Why are you here in a place full of scum?"

"To interrogate Scarface. I had to return my word. He knew what was coming."

"Then, I'm assuming you're aware."

"Aware of what?"

"The Warriors of the Claw."

Terror looked down at the defeated ninjas, seeing the insignia on their attire. He remembered seeing the same mark on his last mission. Nodding to himself, he told Devil-Knight he's seen the mark before. Once hearing those words, Devil-Knight went over the bar and snatched Scarface from the corner, tossing him into one of the chairs nearby. Scarface brushed himself off as Terror and Devil-Knight stood in front of him. Terror's arms were crossed and Devil-Knight's fists were clinched.

"Listen, man. I've told you everything I know."

"Speak it with a little more clarity." Terror said. "We know you have some extra knowledge in that head of yours."

"You know why I came here." Devil-Knight said. "Tell me the name of their master."

"I don't know their master! I only know them when they come in with demands."

"What kind of demands?" Terror asked.

"Things that may give them some leverage in the city. They are here, you know. Dwelling somewhere in Chicago. Moving about like shadows in the night. It is why they came to me. My club keeps their shadows shielded from the light."

"Seems the shadows have an alternate motive." Terror grinned.

Scarface could only stare. Fear held his breath within his throat as Devil-Knight stepped closer. Terror watched on, seeing how Devil-Knight worked in the field. Devil-Knight nodded and raised himself up, stepping back from Scarface.

"He's telling the truth."

"How can you tell?" Terror wondered.

"His heartbeat is sound. Although, there are others things he's guilty of. Yet, those are not what I seek."

"Then, I'll take care of those. Another day."

The two heroes took their leave as Scarface sighed, wiping the sweat from his forehead as he looked around at an empty nightclub with defeated ninjas and knocked around furniture. While they walked, Devil-Knight informed Terror of the Warriors' master and how they need to find whomever it is before it's too late. Terror understood Devil-Knight's keen urgency and walked with him through the night, seeking to learn more about the Warriors of the Claw.

11

THE ORIGIN OF THE CLAW

Devil-Knight and Terror continued their conversation walking through the city. Devil-Knight began to tell him the origins of the Warriors. Stating their purpose is world conquest. Devil-Knight explained how the ninjas were all recruited from different parts of the world. The Claw shows no jurisdiction nor hatred as they believe everyone is capable of being the best only if they're pushed to the exceeded limit. Terror wondered how Devil-Knight knew so much about the Warriors, leading to his answer by stating he was once trained under the study of the Claw.

"Then, you've seen their master." Terror said. "Must have."

"No. I saw lieutenants of lower rank. Masters in the field, but they were not the direct leader. Most of us never saw the master and we often wondered why. All up to this moment, no one has truly met the master. It's a mystery in of itself."

"So, why interrogate ol' Scarface about it if no one's seen the master?"

"To gain more information. Every small bit will eventually lead me to the master. That way, I can get the upper hand and the rest will fall into place."

"How long you've been on this mission of yours?"

"Ever since I came to this city. I already knew it was a place the Warriors had settled in. alongside the news regarding the nubreed population here, it only made their presence remain in darkness. I know of your works with those Yonderers."

"I'm not a member of the team. Only a helping hand."

"So far, I see they haven't had any recent encounters. Makes me wonder are they still in the area."

"Not this time. They're off elsewhere on a recon mission. They'll be back." Terror answered. "They'll have no choice. Chicago is their home. As it is mine."

They walked until reaching the top of a nearby building. Looking out in the distance, Devil-Knight stared, glaring out toward the downtown district of Chicago, seeing the streets and the vehicles passing through. He nodded before turning back to Terror. Terror checked his firearms to dbule0check the ammo. Taking one out as he reloaded the other.

"How often do you use them?" Devil-Knight questioned.

"When I need to. What's the concern? You're not a gunman?"

"Always preferred my fists and feet to do my fighting. It's done me wonders."

"I can believe that. You were trained by ninjas after all." Terror chuckled. "I had a much darker past. Didn't have ninjas help me out. Only a deranged scientist and his cronies of suchlike temperament."

"You speak of Agency X."

"I'm starting to wonder how you know so much about the goings within the city and yet, you've managed to do nothing about them. I see you're only concerned about these Claw Warriors and once you're done with them, you'll return to the shadows."

"That is my mission and my call."

"Well, my mission is to help those in need. Wherever they are."

"You seem like a good man. The city must be proud to have someone like you protecting them."

"Eh, not really. I'm a vigilante in their eyes. No concern to me. But, the job is the job."

"I take it you will aid me on this mission."

"Our missions are aligned. You seek the master. I want to find these Warriors."

Over in the Lincoln Square district, Kang-Zhu arrived in the city. Moving with stealth, he kept to himself as he searched around for any signs of the Warriors. Going from alleyways and streets, Kang-Zhu walked past the entry point of the commercial corridor. Once there, he caught the sound of a strange scream. Making his way toward it, running with such speed, Kang-Zhu stopped as he saw several civilians being held down by five individuals. Kang-Zhu stood his ground as his stance was made known.

"Step back!" Kang-Zhu yelled.

The five strangers each paused and stepped back, giving the civilians way to escape. Once they fled, thanking Kang-Zhu for his appearance, the five strangers turned around to face him. As they turned, Kang-Zhu saw their faces and it only brought him confusion. Keeping his stance, yet with some staggering. The strangers were dressed in raggedy clothing and their faces stuck out like clowns. Eyes darkened by the makeup and smiles were carved across their faces almost as if by a blade. They moved with a slow fashion. Taking each step once at a time. Showing no fear toward Kang-Zhu as his chi imbued from him. The lack of fear within them began to cause a slight stumble on Kang-Zhu, yet, he kept his composure to himself and remained focused.

"You're not Warriors of the Claw."

"No. We are not." One of the strangers said. "We are something else. Something beyond."

"You're not my concern. However, you were seeking o harm innocent people and I cannot allow you to escape."

"You want to face us? All of us?"

"Looks like I have no choice." Kang-Zhu stomped his foot forward. "Make your move."

The strangers ran toward Kang-Zhu as they were shoved back by his chi. He watched as they rose up undamaged and went to strike him again. Hitting them once more with the same blast, they rose up and returned to do the same with laughter screeching from their mouths. Seeing the blast being ineffective, Kang-Zhu sighed and began fighting the strangers with his hands and feet. Attacking them at every angle, only for them to rise up and retaliate with their own attacks of slashing hands and screams of terror with another dose of laughter.

"What are you people made of?" Kang-Zhu questioned within himself, still striking with attacks.

Kang-Zhu held his own in facing them, using his feet to trip them and his hands to impact their chests. He continued fighting them with every attack in his mind, but slowly leaning it was no harm to them. They kept coming. Seeing it become fact as his attacks were not doing any damage to them, the sound of running footsteps sounded off behind him in the street. Turning around f or a split second, he saw two men rushing toward the strangers and fighting back.

"Dante, take those!" said one of the strangers. "I'll handle these three."

"You cannot stop the Circus!" One of the estrangers screamed. "The Circus is eternal!"

"Circus?" Kang-Zhu said.

Kang-Zhu watched as the two allies in the fight came in and quickly decimated the strangers. Kang-Zhu saw the first man take out three of them with one blow as his strength was beyond human. The second man pulled out a sword from his chest and slashed his way through the remaining two before burning their bodies to a crisp with the sword. The strangers were defeated as the two helpers turned toward Kang-Zhu. They measured him, seeing his attire.

"You're not from around here are you?"

"No." Kang-Zhu answered. "I'm not."

"Neither are we. But, here we are."

"Who are you guys anyway?"

"I'm Jack Stone. He's Dante Hale. We're from the East Coast."

"And why are you here in Chicago?"

"Same as you we imagine. You came across those damn ninjas with the claw mark on their outfits?"

"I did. I know of them very well. Almost too well."

"That's good. Because we're here to find them and give them a piece of our mind."

"But, what did they do to you that made you come all the way from the East Coast?"

"They stepped a little too deep into our territory." Dante Hale said. "No one trespasses on our territory."

"No need to get riled up, yet." Stone said. "Save your energy for those ninjas. We know they're somewhere in the city."

"Just your luck, I have a trail on them."

Stone nodded, walking toward Kang-Zhu and extended his hand.

"Looks like we have the same calling."

Kang-Zhu shook his hand in agreement and the three of them went off to find the Warriors of the Claw within the city. Elsewhere in the city, Devil-Knight and Terror continued their conversation on the rooftop. Speaking from topics regarding the nubreeds and the Warriors. Both saw similarities within their own missions and knew what they were doing was the right thing, even with their differences in how to operate. While they conversed, Devil-Knight caught the strange sound in the air above them. Glaring up to Terror's dismay, he clinched his fists and focused in the night sky. Terror looked up, moving is sunglasses.

"What do you see?" Terror asked.

"Not what I see. What I hear. Something's flying above us. Something large."

"You're certain?"

"I always am."

"Ok. Then, can you tell if it's nubreed or machine?"

"Not machine."

"Good to know. Then it's a nubreed."

"No." Devil-Knight said. "Not a nubreed either."

Terror nodded, as he slowly reached toward his side for the gun. He grabbed it and slowly pulled it from its holster. Once the gun was out and raised, the flying sounded increased and rushed toward them from above. Terror gazed up as the flying figure leaped atop him, going for a strike. Devil-Knight moved in with a kick, knocking the creature from Terror's chest. Terror rose from the ground with his gun loaded and began taking shots. The creature dodged the rounds as it twirled and flipped in the air. Devil-Knight looked on toward the creature. Seeing its appearance and eyes. Terror continued firing as quickly as he could.

"The hell is that thing?! A giant owl?!"

"The Death Raptor."

"What's a Death Raptor?" Terror questioned while firing.

The Death Raptor moved through the air, screeching like a roaring horn. Both kept his focus on the creature, seeing it brown feathered presence with its sinister red-yellow eyes. The Death Raptor's size was nearly as large as Terror and Devil-Knight, only with its wingspan surpassing them. The Death Raptor flew toward them, swiping away with its armed claws. The two heroes ducked from every incoming attack with Terror returning the favor with rounds into its wings.

"Aren't you going to do something?" Terror asked.

"I have an idea."

"I'm waiting on it."

Devil-Knight focused his eyes on the Death Raptor and as the creature was coming back in for another swipe, Devil-Knight leaped up and managed to stomp the creature in its back as he flipped himself back onto the roof. Terror watched as the creature stumbled in the air, slowly regaining its flight. Devil-Knight nodded as Terror took the shot, shooting the creature in the head, watching it fall to the pavement. Making their move to see if the creature was dead, they looked and the body had vanished. Confused, Terror wondered if the creature was something of a paranormal nature. Devil-Knight returned to his post unafraid by the creature's sudden vanishing trick. Terror shoved him while pointing toward the spot of the Death Raptor's fall. Nothing came from Devil-Knight and it annoyed Terror.

"Nothing huh."

"There's no need in worrying about the Death Raptor. The job is done."

"And yet the body is gone. You knew of the creature. So, I take it you've had an encounter before."

"I did. Before my arrival to this city."

"Some adventures you've had."

"Wouldn't call them adventures. More like trials. Tests to see if I'm capable of doing what needs to be done."

"And I assume you are since you're here."

"You're learning."

"Good to know."

Devil-Knight looked up toward the sky, noticing the sunrise. He turned to Terror as he saw the sun peaking from the distance.

"Do what you can." Devil-Knight said. "We will meet again."

"What are you talking about? We can do this now."

"I cannot. For the day is near. I must not be out in the light. The shadows are my home. As will they ever be."

"You want me to search during the day, huh?"

"What else are you going to do? This is your mission just as much as it is mine. The city cannot wait any longer and I don't know if there are others who are doing the same. Yet, if they are, we will all meet and end this. But, for now, do your part in it. I will return at nightfall to continue my work."

"Fair point." Terror said, turning around to reload his gun. "Another thing-"

Terror turned back, seeing the Devil-Knight was gone. He sighed, shaking his head in annoyance.

"Just like Swords."

III

ASTONISHING VISITORS

The following day had come, Kang-Zhu walked with Jack Stone and Dante Hale through Uptown. Continuing their own search for the Warriors of the Claw. Finding nothing but dead ends in every corner of their path, Kang-Zhu's source had struck, leading them to a small store somewhere within the district. In finding the store, Kang-Zhu used a device which was given to him by his unknown source. Stone glanced at the device and pulled out his phone, examining them both.

"What's the damn difference?"

"Nothing." Dante said. "They're both tracking devices."

"Hmm." Stone replied. "Fair point."

Upon discovering the location, Kang-Zhu looked at the device as it began to give off a signal. Looking ahead of them, they see they're standing in front of the Uptown Theatre. Stone nodded as he looked down at the device. Hearing the beeping.

"Guess this is the place."

"It is." Kang-Zhu said.

"Might want to put that away now."

Kang-Zhu gave Stone a look. One of watchfulness as they entered the theatre. Walking inside, they quickly noticed there's no one around. Not even employees. Stone searched the area and found no one as did Dante.

"I'm not understanding any of this." Stone said. "How were we able to get in if there's no employees around? Who left the door unlocked?"

"I did." a voice answered from the corner.

The three turned and saw the one who spoke. Wearing his red jacket and jeans. Kang-Zhu raised up the device and the stranger nodded.

"Seems you came. Right on cue."

"Who are you supposed to be?" Stone asked.

"Max Martin. Agent of T.I.T.A.N."

Come again?" Stone said. "Agent of what?"

"Follow me and I'll explain everything."

Kang-Zhu went ahead ad followed Max Martin. Stone nodded as Dante went forward with Stone taking the final steps to follow Martin.

Meanwhile at his base, Terror sat with Jade Horror informing her of his recent encounter with Devil-Knight and the Death Raptor. Jade ha jokingly told Terror she's known of the Death Raptor's existence for some time. Even to the point of being sent on a mission during their early days in Agency X to capture the creature. Terror however was unimpressed to hear of their failure in doing so.

"What's next?" Jade asked.

"I keep doing what I'm doing. Track down any leads I can find and once nightfall comes, he'll be back out there."

"You need any assistance on your part? I could be useful. Other than searching for more leads to finding Mite and his nubreed soldiers. Besides, Carl and Jordan are already on it faster than I go reach."

"No. that cannot go without notice. You handle Mite's whereabouts. I'll deal with this whole ninja thing."

"Well, if anything comes up, contact me."

"I'll be sure to do that." Terror said with a chuckle under his breath.

Back at the Theatre, Max Martin sat with Kang-Zhu, Stone, and Hale as he discussed their reason for meeting him. Primarily Kang-Zhu's reason. Stone interrupted Martin's talk, asking about the strangers they met in the commercial corridor of Lincoln Square. Max went and grabbed a folder from his pile and searched through it. Taking out a sheet of paper, he handed it to Stone.

"What is this?" Stone questioned, looking at the paper.

"It's what you wanted to know. All there is."

Stone glanced at the paper and read the details. He looked up toward Martin and waved the paper around.

"You guys knew about them the whole time?"

"We know what's going on everywhere. T.I.T.A.N. doesn't miss a mark."

"Then, you're aware about the Warriors of the Claw?" Kang-Zhu asked.

"We are. That is why I have to give you this."

Max reached into his bag and took out a cube-like object made of wood with something glowing in the middle. Reflecting the sunlight. Giving it over to Kang-Zhu, he measured it and looked at the markings on the sides before focusing on what was kept inside.

"What's that?" Stone asked.

"It's one of the tools only found in the dojos of the Warriors of the Claw." Kang-Zhu answered.

"And the red object in the center?" Hale pointed. "Looks like a ruby."

"Because it is. Rubies are one of their primary sources of power. They absorb the energy from them and combine it with their chi."

"How the hell does one do that?" Stone wondered. "Do they smash the ruby or hold it close?"

"Little of both. Oftentimes, some crush the ruby and drink it. It's a unknown custom to many cultures. It's how I discovered them to begin with."

"Drinking jewelry." Stone shook his head. "Never knew that was possible."

"This world is different across landscapes." Martin said. "There's things happening that would make even the novice of heroes tremble."

"And how did you fare?" Dante asked. "You seem very young by the sound of it. And appearance."

"I'm young enough to look out of place and to fit in." Martin smiled. "It's a trait it seems."

Stone let out a laugh as Dante glared. The laughter went down as Martin continued his instructions toward Kang-Zhu. Kang-Zhu gave him a nod of clarity and Martin took note of it. In concluding their business,

Martin informed them he had an associate in the city who was doing their part in finding the base of the Warriors. Kang-Zhu smiled hearing the news.

"Once you find anything," Kang-Zhu said.

"I'll send word." Martin nodded. "Trust me on this one."

Elsewhere in the city, Terror and Horror went on a walk together during noon hours. Terror continued to check the time and gaze upward to keep track of the sun's movements. Jade noticed his gazing and tapped his shoulder before pointing toward his watch.

"What about it?"

"Use the watch rather than gazing above."

"I'm aware of what I'm doing. I'm not only checking the sun's movements."

"But, you're searching the nearby buildings to find this Devil-Knight. I thought you said he doesn't appear during the day?"

"He doesn't."

"So, why are you checking the rooftops? Curiosity perhaps?"

"You could say that. I'm not keen on how he works. But, overall he seems like a man who can be trusted."

"And you're having a hard time trusting him or something?"

"No. I just need to know if we're truly working on the same side. No need for it to become a scuffle between the two of us or anyone else who's involved in this mission."

While they walked, Jade placed her arm in front of Terror. Looking at her arm, he turned to her, wondering. He asked her what's the concern. Upon waiting for her to answer, he also sensed something around them. Reaching slowly into his coat for his gun, Jade turned with haste as she was kicked to the ground by Lynch the Hunter, who laughed as he twirled his machete.

"The hell are you?" Terror asked.

"Don't worry about him, fella!" said a voice rushing into Terror, knocking him back. "It's me you need to worry about."

Jade rose up and saw the two attackers as Terror helped her to her feet.

"And these guys are?" Jade questioned.

"I'm not sure about the one who attacked you. But, that one. He's Kane the Mercenary."

"Mercenary, huh? Might be a challenge."

"There's no time for this." Terror raised up his guns and fired.

Lynch dodged the incoming shots as Kane fired back with his own firearms. Jade bolted behind one of the vehicles parked near the sidewalk as Terror fired back against Kane. Lynch saw Jade near the car and grinned, wiping the dripping saliva from his sandy beard. Rushing toward her like a frantic lunatic, he raised the ache te and before he could lower his arm, a lightning bolt struck him against the building nearby. Crashing into the wall. Jade looked out as an arrow pierced through Kane's ballistic armor, holding him into the post which he stood by. Jade stood up from the vehicle and looked at the surroundings. No civilians.

"What did you do?" Terror asked.

"I did nothing. Besides, where did you get arrows from?"

"Wasn't me."

Hearing footsteps approaching them from across the street, the two looked out, seeing Q-Arrow, Voltage, and Bionic Rage. Terror scoffed, giving Jade a look and she knew the kind of expression Terror was feeling.

IV

UNWANTED GUESTS

Over in Uptown, coming into the city was a man, dressed in shiny clothing aside from being shirtless. His sunglasses and hairstyle had to have come from the 1980s as when he walked, bright flashes would emerge from beneath his feet. Startling the civilians as they moved out of his way. He greeted each of them with a smile. The men's faces turned as they saw him aside from the women who began to desire him. Hearing the ring from his phone, he pulled it out and looked, seeing a text message. Taking the moment to read the text, he grinned.

"Ah, so the duo is here. Interesting."

Elsewhere, Terror and Jade had greeted Q-Arrow, Voltage, and Rage. Unusual of them to be in Chicago is what was going through the mind of Terror. Jade had never met them nor any of the other risen heroes since they've appeared throughout the world. The last time Terror saw either of them was when they were all in Enigma City combating the forces of Oranos' Blacholian army. Terror even looked up in the sky to see if they had returned, giving Q-Arrow a reason to laugh.

"You think that's funny?" Terror said.

"There's no ophfiends around here this time. I hope not."

"Then, why are you three here in Chicago? Another mission by Nader or something?"

"No. Not related to Nader or any of that spy business." Q-Arrow answered, holding his bow steady. "We're here because on the same matter. This Claw group running around. Seems they're everywhere."

"You're hunting down these ninjas too?"

"Yeah. They left some of their stuff behind in Vegas. Same with Voltage and Rage. They had a little scuffle with them in their neck-of-the-woods."

"Not exactly a scuffle." Voltage said. "More like an ambush."

"And what have you found so far?" Rage asked Terror.

"I've met the ninjas. Few of them, but I did not take them out. The Devil-Knight did."

"Devil-Knight?" Q-Arrow said. "Never heard of the guy."

"Well, stay put here for the night and you'll meet him."

"He's that kind of guy, huh. Maybe I will. See what he's made of."

Jade went and looked over for the Kane and Lynch, however they were gone. Giving attention to it, the others took notice and searched the surroundings for the two mercenaries. Voltage and Rage went to the rooftops to gain a better look and all of them found nothing. No trace to their sudden escape.

"Well, they are mercenaries." Voltage said. "Don't they know that art of vanishing?"

"Never mind them." Terror said. "They'll pop up again. Probably sooner than we think. Right now, we need to find this ninja clan and get this done."

"Ok." Q-Arrow said. "So, where do we start?"

"Simple. Voltage and Rage can search the city. Split ourselves into teams to gain more cover. Chicago's a big place. So, we really have no choice."

"And what if we come up against these ninjas?" Rage asked. "We take them out or do we bring them in?"

"Do what you must." Terror answered. "Besides, there's more than one of them. Their numbers won't make much difference once we get answers."

"What about me?" Jade asked. "Like I told you, I can help out."

"True. But, who will keep watch over the base and over Carl and Jordan's lives?"

Jade sighed, moving her hair from her eyes.

“Fair point.”

“And what about us?” Q-Arrow questioned. “We just walkthrough the city like some tourists?”

“No. We wait till nightfall.”

“Nightfall? Why would we do that?”

“Because, that’s when he comes out. We’ll need him on this one.”

Back over in Uptown, Kang-Zhu, Stone, and Dante continued walking around. Stone often asked if Kang-Zhu had a car they could ride in and Zhu declined. Stating he’s just a visitor to the city and nothing more. Dante pointed over to a taxi. Stone perceived to take it, although a glistening reflection caught his eye further down the road. Keening his gaze toward it.

“You see that?” Stone asked.

“See what?” Kang-Zhu said, looking in the similar direction.

Dante took several steps ahead and looked. His eyesight was much better than Stone’s. what Dante said was the same individual who entered the city earlier. Lights flashing after each step he took. Dante turned over to Stone and Stone waited for a response. Getting nothing, he turned and took another look. Now, seeing the flashing lights from under the feet, Stone sighed with anger.

“You’re serious.”

“Yeah.” Dante said. “It’s him.”

“Who’s he?” Kang-Zhu wondered, looking out into the street.

Stone and Dante went ahead and began to walk toward the individual with Kang-Zhu following them. Yelling on about the mission regarding the Warriors. Stone did not want to hear any of it, nor did Dante as their focus was set on confronting the individual. Stone stretched and cracked his knuckles as Dante pulled out his sword. They were ready for a fight. The individual stood out and saw the duo approaching. A large smile formed on his face as he applauded their arrival.

“He wasn’t wrong.” The individual said.

“Why are you here?” Stone asked.

“For reasons of my own business.”

"Tell us the truth, Morrison." Dante said. "Why are you here?"

"If you truly wish to know. I'm here on business."

"What kind of business?" Stone questioned. "If you mind us asking."

Their eyes locked on to each other. Two against one as Kang-Zhu made it to them. He stopped in his steps, looking at their stare-down. He could sense some history between the three of them and it appeared to not have gone well. Morrison grinned as he removed his sunglasses, revealing his eyes were lit up like the sun.

"Retribution." Morrison grinned, as his eyes flashed before them.

The bright flash was powerful enough to stop traffic on the roads and to even blind the civilians who were nearby. Stone, Dante, and Kang-Zhu covered their eyes from the flash as Morrison only laughed before blasting the two allies with a surge of static energy. Knocking them off their feet in their temporary blindness, Morrison continued the attack. Kang-Zhu calmed himself and stood still. The chi within him began to charge up and from his abdomen, the chi made itself known to Morrison. Glowing like a rising sun, the chi went up from his stomach and chest to his eyes, restoring the temporal blindness. Kang-Zhu's focus was from observation to defensive as he retaliated with an energy blast of his own, striking Morrison in the chest with a punching blow.

"Goddamn!" Morrison yelled. "You're one strong son-of-a-bitch!"

"It's a given trait."

"How are you at perception?"

"What do you mean?" Kang-Zhu wondered.

The sound of a sniper echoed through the streets as Kang-Zhu turned around. The sense of urgency looming over his shoulders as he gazed upward and within the air, he felt a presence of familiarity. Glaring closer, he raised his arm and his hand opened. Within that moment, Kang-Zhu snatched a round from the air, surprising Morrison and the shooter who watched from above. Staring out through an open window.

"Damn, you're good!" Morrison said.

"Who's with you?" Kang-Zhu asked. "Are you working with the Warriors of the Claw?"

"The Warriors of what? I have no idea what you're talking about, boy."

“Then I’ll have to beat some answers out of you.”

Kang-Zhu went for another strike, only for the pavement in front of him to spark by the impact of another bullet. Pausing himself, he turned back and looked up to the window, seeing the shooter in detail.

“You have friends I see.”

“He’s not exactly a friend.” Morrison said. “More like a partner in a certain cause.”

Swinging down from the window to the road was a mercenary. Stone and Dante from that moment began to regain their sight, still somewhat blurry from the flash. Yet, it was clear enough for Stone to get a good look toward Morrison as he bum-rushed over and speared him to the ground. While Stone and Morrison had their conflict, the mercenary landed on the ground and aimed his rifle once more toward Stone. Kang-Zhu went to stand in the way, only for Dante to move him from the path.

“What are you doing?”

“Just watch.” Dante said with a grin.

The mercenary took the shot and the bullet mad e its move toward Stone’s back. Passing in between Dante and Kang-Zhu, the bullet hit Stone’s back and fell to the concrete. Stone paused for a moment before punching Morrison in the face and tossing him several feet from them down the road. The mercenary was astounded by Stone’s strength. Kang-Zhu was also impressed. Staring at Stone as he walked past him.

“How did you?” Kang-Zhu wondered.

“Impenetrable skin.” Stone said. “It’s a habit.”

Stone stepped forward to face the mercenary. He scoffed as the mercenary began to load up another round into the rifle.

“You’re first shot didn’t work! What makes you think the second one will?”

“Give it up, Deadon.” Dante said. “You’ve lost this one.”

“I never lose.” Deadon said. Aiming the rifle.

V

GROWING CONFLICT

Deadon aimed and took the second shot. The round went forth and as Kang-Zhu charged up, Dante held his sword steady, and Stone stood still. The bullet was incepted in the air by a rushing naginata. The bladed staff struck into concrete with the bullets caught in between them. Everyone stood at a standstill while from around the corner emerged Gozen. She looked at Kang-Zhu and nodded. Picking up her weapon, she gave Deadon a stare and he was uncertain to reload. Yet, he did and took another shot. Only for the third round to be slashed in half by Gozen's quick reflexes.

"Want to take another shot?" Gozen said.

Deadon took a moment and lowered the rifle. Taking out a smaller handgun, he fired it into the building nearby and grappled into the air, vanishing from the scene. Gozen watched as he fled and sighed. Turning around to Kang-Zhu, Stone, and Dante, she smiled.

"Told you I would be here."

"I take it you know something about these ninjas?" Stone asked.

"I know where they are."

Stone looked at Dante who turned to Kang-Zhu.

"Where are they?" Kang-Zhu asked.

Throughout the remainder of the day, Voltage and Rage went through the entire city of Chicago to the surprising sight of the residents. Knowing of the two heroes, yet not ever seeing them due to their base of operations in other larger cities across the country. Upon their search, they discovered nothing in which related to the Warriors of the Claw. Once they took a moment to relax, Voltage looked up to the sky and noticed the sunset beginning. Raising up from his seat atop a building.

"Looks like our work is about to begin."

"Meaning what?" Rage asked.

"Sunset's coming."

"As it always does. What's the concern?"

"You heard Terror about that Devil-Knight guy."

"I did. Are you in fear of him or something?"

"No. I just want to be sure we don't miss out on anything."

Rage nodded as he stood up and stretched his bionic limbs, surprising Voltage that they're even capable of stretching. Rage shook his head as the sound of metal clashing caught their attention. Walking over toward the edge of the building, they looked out and saw the ninjas fighting against four figures.

"We should go." Voltage said, bolting away.

"Took my words, kid." Rage replied, flying after him.

Reaching the location, Voltage and Rage saw the ninjas fighting against Kang-Zhu, Gozen, Stone, and Dante. Landing on the ground at the same time to their own amusement, they ran in and aided the four heroes against the Warriors. Voltage blasted them with his lighting as Rage went ahead and fired shotgun rounds from his bionic arms. While the two helped out, Stone stepped back and admired Rage's bionic limbs while Dante didn't know what to make of them.

"Who are these guys?" Dante wondered.

Rage took the final shot, killing the remaining ninja. Upon turning around, they approached each other to their own surprise. Stone only could stare at Rage's arms, reaching out to touch them. Rage pulled back.

"Sorry. I'm just checking out your arms. Wow! Where'd you get them?"

"Military experiment. Nothing else."

"I'm sorry, but who are you two?" Kang-Zhu asked.

"I'm The Astonishing Voltage and he is Dameon Mason. Or as the people of Detroit call him, the Bionic Rage."

"Alright, that's enough."

"Hold on." Stone said. "You're the guy from Detroit? The one who took down Spencer Vargas?"

"How do you know about Vargas?"

"Dante and I had a run-in with some of his men during one of our alley brawls back in the East Coast. We never met Vargas. Although, we hear he's in prison. So, I guess that's good enough."

"For his sake, I hope he stays there." Rage said, reloading his arms."

"Why are you two here in Chicago?" Gozen questioned. "Are you searching for the Warriors of the Claw as well?"

Rage sighed, turning the attention toward Voltage as he walked off.

"As a matter of fact, we are. I guess after what just happened, you're all here for the same reason."

"Yes." Gozen replied. "I have a clue to their base. It's precisely in the Loop district of this city."

"Then let's get going." Kang-Zhu said.

"Wait." Voltage paused. "Can I offer a suggestion, if you don't mind."

"What kind of suggestion?" Gozen questioned.

"We should inform the others."

"There's more?" Stone said. "How many more have the ninjas messed with."

"Plus, nightfall is nearing." Voltage mentioned while gazing up. "Only a matter of time before he arrives."

"Who's he?" Kang-Zhu said.

"The Devil-Knight."

Stone was still. Dante was silent. Gozen was unbothered. Kang-Zhu was curious, yet frozen. Their posture was like a still painting with only their expression to tell the tale. Voltage nodded as he waved his hands.

"I know, you haven't heard of the guy. Neither did I until we came here. Terror told us he only comes out at night and he has great information on the Warriors of the Claw. We need to meet with him."

Gozen looked at Kang-Zhu with a nod of solidarity. Stone and Dante agreed with their decision. Voltage even nodded, just to nod.

In another part of Chicago, Terror and Q-Arrow stood atop the same rooftop he last saw Devil-Knight. The night had come, they waited. Q-

Arrow yawned as he glanced down at a watch, he wore on his utility belt.

"Ok, when is this guy going to show up?" Arrow wondered.

"Give him a moment."

"We've been on this roof for nearly three hours. Where else is the guy going to show up?"

"You seek for me." Devil-Knight asked, standing before them both to Terror's amusement.

"This the guy?" Arrow said. "This him?"

"Yes, this is him." Terror nodded. "Good of you to meet with me again. I'm sure you've discovered something I have not."

"I have learned of a particular ploy in this mission. An associate to the Warriors of the Claw."

"An associate?" Arrow said. "Who's the suspect?"

"Some organization calling themselves the Circus. I believe them to be working with the Warriors of the Claw."

"Any chance on their base?" Terror asked. "Figured that would be the spot to get them all in one place."

"I have not. Not yet."

"Alright then." Arrow said. "Now, what is the next plan? We contact the others and all meet up somewhere?"

"Sounds good to me." Terror answered. "What about you? Willing to tag alone with a few of us to end this mission of ours?"

"Are these others capable of a challenge such as this?"

"I believe they are." Terror said. "Plus, I have seen it for myself."

Devil-Knight nodded as he gazed p to the moon, hearing the horns of vehicles below in the distance. Q-Arrow's face cringed as his eyes looked over to Terror. Terror shook his head as Devil-Knight turned back to them.

"Very well. The night is young. Let's finish all of this before daybreak."

"Wait. What? You want to get this done before sunrise/ how are we ever going to get that done so quickly?"

"Because we make moves." Terror said. "And moves bring results."

Terror agreed with Devil-Knight and Q-Arrow followed as they left the rooftop and went out to meet the others in the city.

VI

THE PLAY

Over in the Loop district, the Warriors themselves gathered in an underground location. Within the room which resembled an old parking garage or a place once used for docking supplies as their laid scraps of papers with company logos across them, they stood. Patiently. Single-filed lines throughout the damp, cold room. What they faced was a door. At the count of three in their minds, the door opened and entering the room was a man who looked as if he just came out of a circus. Or fired from one. His eyes were chaotic as his smile stretched across his cheeks. The drapes of his long black hair mixed with the atmosphere of the room.

"I see he's kept his words." The man said. "Good. I am aware none of you know who I am. But, your master has given me instruction to command you in this quest we've constructed. I am the Jester and out there, my Circus is currently operating the tactics for your procedure of call. When you see them out there, do not make a move on them. For they work in your best interest. As they work in favor of yours."

The Warriors gave the Jester a nod of their agreement. The grin on Jester's face grew to an increase in such a manner a smile should not form on a human face. Clapping his hands and let out a chilling laugh, one in which would make even the serious of men tremble.

"Finally." The Jester spoke. "Which our combined effort, we will bring that cursed Devil-Knight into the light for all of the world to see. Only then, will he understand that his methods are false. A new dawning is near."

Coming near the Loop district, Gozen, Kang-Zhu, Stone, and Dante made their arrival. Following Gozen around as she led them to the precise location she discovered, they come to a stop in South Loop.

"Is this the spot?" Stone asked while his eyes wandered.

Gozen's eyes searched the surroundings. Looking at the spot, she noticed a railroad track. Her eyes widen with a snap of her fingers, she pointed.

"This is the spot. Now, only to find the exact location."

"We're in the spot?" Dante asked. "And where is their entrance? Wouldn't expect it be above ground to start with."

"You figured it out." Gozen smiled. "There. That doorway should lead into an underground warehouse."

"How do you know there's a warehouse under here?" Kang-Zhu questioned. "I'm not sure there is."

"Things are rarely revealed to everyone. Not a secret if they aren't."

Stone and Dante went for the door and upon Stone's hand being pressed against the handle, the door shattered open. Shoving Stone back into Dante as Gozen and Kang-Zhu looked on, seeing the Warriors coming out of the door like rats from a sewer. However, alongside them were the individuals like the ones Kang-Zhu came into conflict upon his arrival. He recognized their marks across their faces. Scars and paint. Like roughed-up clowns.

"More of them."

"Of who?" Gozen asked, raising up her naginata.

"Them." Kang-Zhu said. "I encountered some during my arrival."

"Just in the street?"

"They were attacking civilians. I couldn't resist the fight."

"Well, guess you can fight them again. Only with me at your side."

The entire area became a place of an all-out brawl. Stone and Dante took the fight to the five Warriors while Kang-Zhu and Gozen leaped into battle with the clowns of the Circus. Stone being a brawler, used his punches and weigh against the Warriors' own combative strikes. Dante took out his sword and slashed through two of them within seconds, impressing even himself.

"You're good over there, Jack?"

"I'm doing well." Stone answered while punching one of the Warriors in the nose. "Easy business."

Nearly finished with the fights, a blast of wind blew from the opened door, gathering their attention. Even the remaining Warriors and Circus clowns came to a pause. Everyone stared at the door, seeing something blowing to the outside from within. Gozen twirled the naginata as she stepped forward before swiping one of the clowns with the handle of the naginata.

"What is that?" She questioned as the wind intensified.

Through the rushing wind appeared a cloaked figure. The face shrouded by the darkly hood as he levitated out into the open. Pausing on the outside as the door shut behind them. Stone and Dante looked at one another with confusion. Gozen stood her ground with Kang-Zhu slowly charging himself up as orbs emerged from his hands.

"It appears we have some disturbance in our plot." The cloaked one said.

"I guess you're their leader." Gozen said.

"Not their leader, no. more like an influencer of the mind and the spirit."

"Hey," Stone said. "what's with the hood and cape?"

"Allow me to introduce myself."

The hood flowed with the wind, revealing the figure's face to be a skull. Not of human appearance in detail, yet with jagged edges and wider eyes. The pupils glared like the stars as a dark grin formed on his face.

"I am Sinister Fear and this is your end."

Sinister Fear raised his hands and from his fingertips speared daggers of solid darkness. Gozen deflected the daggers with heir naginata as Kang-Zhu charged up and blasted a chi-blast toward Fear, who evaporated out of the blast's path before reforming behind Kang-Zhu. Swiping the young martial artist down, Gozen went for a strike as Fear blocked the attack in the air with a shield of solid shadow. Gozen struggled to get the hit. Stone and Dante rushed in to aid her with punches and strikes from Dante's sword. None of the attacks proved useful as Fear sighed and swiped his hand, transforming the shield into a blast, knocking the three heroes to the ground with a force as powerful as an explosion.

"Puny in their strength. Yet, their minds are strong. Only with fear will they be consumed. However, this moment is not the accurate time."

Through a cloud of shadows did Sinister Fear and the remaining Warriors disappear.

Over in another district nearly close to the Loop, Devil-Knight, Terror, and Q-Arrow through his contacts met up with Voltage and Rage. Voltage remained paused by Devil-Knight's appearance as Rage was calm.

"This the guy?" Rage said.

"He is." Terror replied. "Find anything out there?"

"Nothing." Rage answered. "Not even a glimmer of ninjas."

"Yet, someone has." Devil-Knight said, looking in the distance.

"Who's this someone?" Q-Arrow questioned.

"Four others. They've found the entrance."

"Who are the other four?" Terror asked. "Who else is in this city?"

"Hold on." Rage said. "How does he know if there are others?"

"I can sense their essence in the air. It's drawing me to them. Our purposes are aligned."

"That' s an interesting power trait." Voltage pointed.

Devil-Knight continued his gaze and pointed eastward.

"There. This is where we must go."

"And you're certain of this?" Q-Arrow wondered. "We're supposed to take your word?"

"Do you have any other options?" Devil-Knight grinned.

"He smiles." Voltage said. "Oh, that's good to know."

"We'll follow your lead." Terror said.

VII

ANSWERS

Terror, Voltage, Q-Arrow, and Rage followed Devil-Knight through the city, trusting in his instincts as he led them wherever he sensed. Entering the Loop district and heading into the direction of South Loop, over ahead Devil-Knight pointed.

"There."

Terror looked out and saw four figures on the ground.

"Are they alive?"

"Yes." Devil-Knight said. "We need to speak with them. As they need to regain their strength."

"What happened to them?" Q-Arrow wondered.

"They were attacked."

"By what?"

"A shadow of a kind. A sinister one."

They ran over and found Kang-Zhu, Gozen, Stone, and Dante on the ground. Seeking to wake them up as Devil-Knight's focus was set on the dented door. Terror knelt and revived Gozen.

"I've seen you before, haven't I?" Terror asked.

"Not exactly. Although you've worked with a close friend of mine."

"A friend?" Terror wondered.

"You'll figure it out."

Terror nodded. Q-Arrow and Rage helped Stone and Dante to their feet as Voltage helped Kang-Zhu.

"You're a ninja too?" Voltage asked.

"Not in full. What happened to us?"

"You were all taken out by Sinister Fear." Devil-Knight said. "I was unaware of his arrival."

"Yeah." Gozen said, stretching her arm. "We saw him. He came through the door."

"I see. Then, you've discovered the lair of the Warriors."

"Yes. I did."

"We need to enter now."

"Hold on." Q-Arrow said. "We need to give these guys some rest. They were just attacked."

"We don't have any more time. This is the entrance to their lair. Therefore, we must enter it and end all of this before they grow in numbers."

"I agree." Gozen said, grabbing her weapon from the ground. "I'm in favor of some payback."

"Aren't we all." Kang-Zhu said. "Let's finish this."

Devil-Knight nodded and Terror agreed.

VIII

SPIRITUAL INTERFERENCE

In a dimension completely shrouded in darkness, Sinister Fear sat in a sphere mixed with dimmed light and flowing darkness. His eyes were closed as he began reciting a ritual. One of a demonic nature. In speaking the ritual in an old language not known to the modern world, in front of him formed a glyph made of hellfire. The shadowed dimension transformed into a burning blue glow as within the glyph formed a disembodied spirit.

"You have summoned me." The spirit said.

Sinister Fear's eyes opened, seeing the spirit. Taking a moment, he stood up as the sphere shattered into smoke. Bowing before the spirit, the spirit stopped him before he could reach the ground.

"I am not a lord. Therefore, do not treat me as such."

"Very well. You are the Phantom of Sin, correct?"

"I am."

"I know of your past experience with the Death Chaser and his allies in the spiritual arts."

"What are you asking of me to do?"

"I require your assistance. Not against enemies in your own field, but heroes of this modern world. Modern gods to humanity. Several seek to ruin a plot myself and my partners have in transforming this world into a realm of darkness. I've learned all I could pertaining to these risen heroes and what I've learned, they've never come into conflict with a being of your kind."

"You believe I will be an asset to your cause and bring forth a new era of darkness?"

"I do. That is why I summoned you this day. Will you align with us and finish these heroes off?"

The Phantom took a moment to pause. With a nod and a glimmer in his shadowed eyes he accepted. Fear nodded as the Phantom disappeared through the blue flames and the dimension returned to its darkened state. Afterwards, Sinister Fear lifted his arms, disappearing once more through a cloud of shadows.

IX

ONE STOP TO THE PIT

Entering the dented door, the heroes walked down a long corridor which smelled of the waters of Lake Michigan. The further they went down, the scent of burning flesh consumed the air. Voltage covered his face with his hand as the stench intensified after every step they took. Q-Arrow did the same. He glanced over to the others, seeing hem unfazed by the smell.

"You're kidding me, right."

"Don't worry." Terror said. "I've dealt with similar stenches before in my time. My nose is used to it."

"Good for you."

Once the light from the outside was unable to enter, candles filled the corridor against eh walls. Gozen noticed the candles were not the modern style many used, yet they appeared to be much older. So much so that Devil-Knight began speaking words in Old English, confusing the others as if they assumed he was speaking to them. Devil-Knight raised his hand as they came to a stop in front of two tall doors. Each on them were inscriptions written in peculiar runes. Gozen approached the door, staring at the markings.

"I'm not familiar with these glyphs."

"I am." Devil-Knight said. "They're demonic in nature."

Placing his hand against the door, Devil-Knight could feel the trembling on the other side. Even hearing the voices of many chanting a name. a name he did not know.

"They're here." Devil-Knight said. "They're all here."

"All the Warriors of the Claw?" Kang-Zhu questioned. "All of them are behind these doors?"

"Yes. Although, our numbers are outmatched. From what I can sense, there appear to be over two dozen of them behind these doors alongside more of those clowns."

"Just our luck." Stone said.

"Very well." Terror spoke. "We take our chances. Make our moves so that we overcome them. Should be simple enough with all of our abilities combined."

"So, you're all ready for the moment you've been heading towards?"

"I am." Terror said, cocking his gun.

"So am I." Gozen answered, holding the naginata.

"I'm with them." Voltage said. "Besides, they jumped me already. This is payback time."

"If it's for the greater good," Rage said. "Then, let's kick down these doors and finish this."

Stone and Dante nodded.

"Let's get to it." Stone answered.

Devil-Knight gave them a nod and pressed forward the door. As it opened, they saw the Warriors of the Claw standing firm with the Circus on their left. In front of both groups were Sinister Fear and the Jester. Looking out toward the door, Sinister Fear grinned while Jester laughed.

"Good." Sinister Fear smiled. "You've come to meet your end."

"I don't think we'll be meeting our end this night." Devil-Knight replied.

"Ah!" Jester jumped. "You've finally come out of the shadows and into our marvelous light."

"You've been searching for me?"

"I have. For a very, very long time."

"Then, you have no worries when I finish you off."

"Oh! Do come and try! For this night is a special one. Isn't that right, Fear-Monger."

"With everything in place and our legions aligned, we will wipe out these heroes who stand before us and usher in a new era of darkness for all the world to witness. Staring first will be this city's end."

Terror raised his gun and fired a shot, killing one of the clowns through the head.

"Only thing ending today is all of this bullshit taking place in my city."

Sinister Fear raised his arms, shouting toward the Warriors to begin their attack against the heroes. Jester leaped around as he directed the circus to do the same. The heroes were prepared as their weapons were drawn and their powers began emitting.

"Let's end this quickly." Devil-Knight said. "Before daybreak."

X

CHICAGO'S END

The battle had commenced within the lair of the Warriors as the heroes clashed with the Warriors and the Circus. Through the ongoing battle, Devil-Knight moved with a much quicker speed than he showed before, impressing Terror and the others. Gozen twirled the naginata, slashing off the heads of clowns and ninjas. Her eyes glared toward Sinister Fear as he let out a chuckle.

"Don't let your sheep fight a wolf alone! Come down here and face me!"

"You seek to challenge my power?"

"What else is there for you to do?"

The Jester laughed as Sinister Fear leaped from the raised ground and crashed in front of Gozen with his hands imbued in an energetic shadow. Going in for a swipe to the head, Sinister Fear blocked the attack and swiped his right hand, tossing Gozen against the brick wall. Over on the other side of the room, Stone and Dante fought off the other Warriors while Voltage and Rage took to the air, blasting the ground with lightning blasts and grenades. The Jester went and sat down in one of the nearby wooden chairs. Leaning back as the ongoing battle happened before him. While he sat, one of Voltage's lightning bolts crashed near his feet, causing him to leap up in defense. As he did, Rage appeared from the other side, spearing the Jester into the wall.

"Stay down." Rage said, aiming his muzzle toward Jester's face.

"You won't kill me, will you? You have heart. Compassion! I can feel it flowing through your very soul."

"I've killed less in many ways. I can kill another if need be."

Seeing the Warriors and Circus nearly being defeated by the combined effort of the heroes. Sinister Fear mumbled under his breath as Gozen attacked him with her weapon, getting a hit. Slashing his chest with the naginata. Sinister Fear stepped back, holding his chest. Gozen grinned.

"Take a look."

He looked down, seeing his own blood coming from the cut. Blood black as a shadow. Growling under his breath as Gozen went on about aiming for his limbs and head. His eyes went solid black, raising his arms to the ceiling.

"You didn't think we would have backup."

While looking at Sinister Fear, a shadow swooped past Gozen. Trying to catch it, Sinister Fear kicked Gozen in her back. Turning around to retaliate, the shadow emerged and snatched Gozen by her throat, slamming her to the floor. Fully emerging from the darkness, the Sin Phantom made itself known.

"And he's not the only one." Sinister Fear said, as from the entrance flown in the Death Raptor. Hearing the sound of the wings, Terror looked up and sighed. Devil-Knight also had done the same with the two heroes turning to each other.

"Thought it was dead." Terror said.

"As did I."

The Death Raptor proved itself for revenge as he swooped down and swiped its claws toward Terror and Devil-Knight. Ducking from the incoming attack, the two heroes began plotting a diversion to strike Death Raptor from the sky. In making their plan, they leaped up and Terror reached into his coat.

"Haven't used this in a while."

Terror reached in and raised up his sword. The Death Raptor turned around heading for them and Terror ran toward the flying creature, leaping into the air as he slashed the wing of the Death Raptor, causing it to crash into the brick wall. Devil-Knight felt a sense in the air, looking up.

"Daybreak is nearing. We need to get this done!"

The Sin Phantom overtook Gozen in a fear of strength. While she was down, the Sin Phantom went into a strike into her chest. Before he could make the attack, a blast of chi came from behind him as Kang-Zhu intercepted the attack. Helping her up, they looked around, seeing Voltage and Rage defeating the remaining Warriors as the Circus was taken out with ease. Looking to the front, they saw the Jester slowly regaining his strength as he rose up from Rage's spear. The Sin Phantom reappeared in front of them like a ghost with a dark laugh as Sinister fear stood next to him, glowing with shadow energy.

"What's next?" Kang-Zhu questioned.

Taking their stance for another fight, the sound of rushing flames roared from the corridor, ceasing the actions of everyone. Sin Phantom hard the sound and quickly moved back, surprising even Sinister Fear by his actions.

"What are you doing?" Sinister Fear questioned.

"It's him. He's here."

From the doors busted in with sinfire, the Death Chaser. His flaming eyes glaring toward everyone as they moved toward the direction of the Sin Phantom. His arm raised, pointing.

"I've come for you."

The Death Raptor had rose up and flown toward the Death Chaser. Unmoved by the coming creature, the chaser raised his left hand and blasted the Death Raptor with a burst of sinfire, causing he creature to turn into ash. The Sin Phantom watching it take place, screamed with fury as he went in for an attack, only for the Death Chaser to grab him by his throat.

"Return to the void where you belong."

The sinfire sparked from the Chaser's hand as he consumed the Sin Phantom into ember. Sinister Fear watched with more anger than before. Stomping his foot, creating a wave of shadow energy to move past the Chaser. Still unmoved.

"I will not be defeated!"

Sinister Fear levitated toward the Chaser and struck with a shadow blast. The Chaser, being unharmed shook off the attack as the sinfire emerged from his body, burning off the remains of the shadow energy.

"That is not possible."

"You've trespassed your boundaries, Fear-Monger.

The Chaser swiped his hands as a portal of sinfire emerged from behind Sinister Fear. Looking back as the heat was greatly intensified. More so than the average fires of the earth. seeking to attack the Chaser again, Devil-Knight leaped in and kicked Sinister Fear in the face with a super kick, causing the fear-monger to fall into the portal.

"This is not over!" Sinister Fear screamed. "I will return!"

"And I will be waiting." Devil-Knight replied as the Chaser sealed it.

The room became silent as from the ceiling, a voice echoed, and a blurry astral figure appeared from the higher ground where Sinister Fear and the Jester stood. Gaining the attention of all the heroes, including the Chaser. The astral figure stared. Its' eyes locked on the Chaser and Devil-Knight in particular.

"You have won this bout. You've defeated my Warriors of my Claw. A tremendous effort on your part. But beware, a greater battle is coming, and it will prove to your downfall."

"Let it come." Devil-Knight said. "I will be there to stop it."

"Hmm. We shall see."

The figure evaporated into nothingness as the heroes took their victory. Seeing the room filled with the bodies of the Warriors and the Circus, they looked over to the front as they realized the Jester was gone. Seeking to find him, the Chaser bid his farewell, disappearing into a portal of sinfire.

Seeing the fight was over and the Warriors were defeated, the heroes returned to the outside just as the sun began to rise over the horizon. From that moment, Voltage, Rage, Q-Arrow, Stone, Dante, Kang-Zhu, and Gozen took their leave as other duties had called for their assistance. Leaving Terror and Devil-Knight remaining. Chicago is their city. Their home.

"I must ask." Terror said. "What will you do now that the battle is won?"

"I will seek out their leader. His name I do not know, but by his words, I can sense he'll be around very soon."

"And when that day comes, I'll be willing to tag along."

Devil-Knight nodded as the sunrise grew. Taking his leave, Terror called out to him, asking if they'll cross paths before the next battle. Devil-Knight gave him a smirk.

"When the times comes, I will be around."

The Devil-Knight took his leave and vanished from Terror's eyes like a blinking light. Terror sighed, placing his sword into his coat as he walked off from the Loop district, returning to his base for another day.

NEXT BOOK IN

THE DARK TITAN UNIVERSE SAGA....

MAGICKS & MYSTICISM

A BOOK RETURNING TO THE SUPERNATURAL LANDSCAPE OF THE DARK TITAN UNIVERSE.

ABOUT THE AUTHOR

Ty'Ron W. C. Robinson II is the author of several works of fiction. Including the *Dark Titan Universe Saga*, *The Haunted City Saga*, *EverWar Universe*, *Symbolum Venatores*, *Frightened!*, *Instincts*, *Chevah Mythos*, *The Horde*, *Argoron*, *The Supreme Pursuer*, *Vanok*, *Dark Titan's The Dead Days*, and *Agent Trevor*.

Also of other books (*The Book of The Elect*, *etc.*) and One-Shot short stories.

More information pertaining to the author and stories can be found at darktitanentertainment.com.

Twitter: @TyRonRobinsonII
Vero: @tyronrobinsonii

Twitter: @DarkTitan_
ıstagram: @darktitanentertainment
Facebook: @DarkTitanEnt

www.ingramcontent.com/pod-product-compliance
Lightning Source LLC
Chambersburg PA
CBHW020524310726
48979CB00014B/2204/J
9781737614333